CW00500281

The Quiet Ones

Betsy Reavley

Copyright © 2016 Betsy Reavley

The right of Betsy Reavley to be identified as the Author of the Work has been asserted by her in accordance Copyright, Designs and Patents Act 1988.
First published in 2016 by Bloodhound Books
Apart from any use permitted under UK copyright law, this publication may only be reproduced, stored, or transmitted, in any form, or by any means, with prior permission in writing of the publisher or, in the case of reprographic production, in accordance with the terms of licences issued by the Copyright Licensing Agency.
All characters in this publication are fictitious and any resemblance to real persons, living or dead, is purely coincidental.

For Trinidad and Stephen

& my brother, Harry.

Writing has laws of perspective, of light and shade just as painting does or music. If you are born knowing them, fine. If not, learn them. Then rearrange the rules to suit yourself.

Truman Capote

I swear from the bottom my heart I want to be healed. I want to be like other men, not this outcast whom nobody wants.

E.M.Forster

Introduction

Every step I take seems to be in slow motion, almost as if it's happenin' to someone else. The thump from the door as I close it behind me sounds muffled and distant. The smell from the alcohol and bleach still lingers, stingin' my nose.

I watch myself take a large stride away from the house where all that filth took place. I'm not leavin' until it's all over - until every last thing has turned to dust.

I sit down on the cold, damp, concrete curb opposite, with my arms folded across my chest and my legs stretched out into the narrow street. Bein' out in the open feels cathartic. This place isn't my home but it might as well be since I don't have one. I live in the shadows, the place where guilt and anger converge.

London is strangely calm and quiet or maybe that's just how it seems to me. Next to the growin' angry flames, everythin' else fades into insignificance. It occurs to me that the houses either side might burn down. But I shrug it off. What does it matter? No one's fuckin' innocent. Not really.

For a moment, I look up at the sky. It's clean and white. The rain has gone, leavin' a soggy world behind. It looks like snow might be in the January air. It's cold enough. At least it would be, if it weren't for the burnin' building opposite.

The speed at which the flames lick up the walls smotherin' everythin' is the loveliest thing I've ever seen. I can't take my eyes off the fire. So many colours. Whoever knew destruction could be so beautiful?

I slip my hand into my black nylon jacket pocket and fumble with the box of matches. An erection stirs. The noise the match made when I struck it was hypnotic. The way it burst into life. Somethin' born out of nothin'. Like me.

I'm watchin' the heat warp the glass in the front window. The pressure builds before it smashes and flames burst through, feedin' off the fresh air and climbin' further up the brick to reach the lip of the roof. It's as if the fire has hands. It searches every surface, feelin' where to go next.

The noise is deafenin'. The crackle of wood, the breakin' glass, the meltin' screams of other unknown fabrics all sing together like a choir while the roar conducts the tune. And somewhere in the distance, I hear the faint wail of sirens. I knew she'd call the police. I've been expectin' them.

Maybe I should have killed her. It would have been good to watch her bleed. But it's too late now. That ship has sailed. I suppose I could run and save myself. But I can't tear myself away from watchin' it all comin' to an end. I've got nowhere left to run. I'm too tired, now. Tired of hidin'. The police are gettin' closer. I can hear them. This is where it ends. But to understand how I ended up here, you'll need to go back to the beginnin'.

Closin' my eyes for a moment, I relish the burnin' heat on my face. It wasn't meant to end like this but life has a funny way of surprisin' you.

The sirens are so close now. I can almost see them. Openin' my eyes again to have one last look, somethin' grabs my attention. A large puddle on the tarmac by my boot is movin'. I look at my reflection in the water but see someone else lookin' back. A less good version of the person I wanted to be.

February 3rd

The phone rings and I know it's her. I push my chair away from my desk putting distance between my body and the telephone. Frozen and staring wide-eyed, the shrill sound grows louder. Charlie pokes his head around the doorframe and looks at me. He has a tea towel in his hands and is wiping a white plate. I shake my head. He nods and returns to the kitchen. The phone continues to jangle. It seems never-ending, but eventually stops.

My legs feel like jelly as I get up and go into the kitchen. Charlie is standing over the sink with his back to me. By the shape of his shoulders, the angle of his head, I can tell he's deep in thought. He's a tall man with a thick head of dark curly hair, grey around the temples. He senses me and turns round. As I approach him, he stretches out his arms and wraps them around me. I feel safe again. He smells like washing up liquid and freshly baked biscuits and I bury my face in the woollen fabric of his cable-knit jumper. His large hands are damp and I feel the wetness soaking through the clothes on my back.

I don't know if I'm angry or scared. Probably both. Pulling away from Charlie, I wander over to the fridge and open the door. I'm hit by the pungent smell of ripe Brie. I really should get round to clearing out the fridge. In the fruit and veg drawer, there are some wrinkled carrots and a manky lettuce that really belong in the bin. Tomorrow, I tell myself as I remove two cold bottles of beer and silently hand one to Charlie. He winks, accepts the drink before turning to fiddle about in one of the kitchen drawers, looking for the ever-elusive bottle opener. He finds it and cracks open his bottle. An eruption of creamy, frothy bubbles spills out over the glass neck and slides down the frosted green sides before pooling on the stone kitchen floor. Neither of us makes a move to clean it up. He passes me the souvenir bottle opener we bought on holiday in Barcelona, and I pop the top off my drink. The serrated metal teeth clang onto the floor and the top spins haphazard, to settle under one of the cupboards.

Charlie sits on a green, painted farmhouse chair at the old pine table. I notice the paint is chipped around the chair legs and make a mental note to touch it up at some point, another job that's bound to be forgotten.

'You'll have to answer at some point, Jo.'

Charlie peels the corners of the label away from the bottle. His brow is furrowed and he looks very serious.

'I don't have to.'

I look down at my feet and think about changing my nail varnish colour. That bluey-pink isn't really my shade.

'You know you do, and the sooner the better.'

The statement hangs in the air.

I feel his large brown eyes searching my face and I look up. Most of the time, I don't notice the age gap between us. It's only seventeen years but tonight he looks somehow older than I'm used to.

'What sort of shape could our relationship possibly take? Too much has happened ...'

'Make room.' He says, knowing it will irritate me.

'*Make room*? It's not a piece of bloody furniture we're discussing.'

He's not going to let this go I think and sigh. I tip the remaining beer into my mouth, letting the cold bubbles fizz down my throat.

'It's only been a few weeks.'

'OK,' he smiles, 'But know that when you do, I am beside you.'

'I know and thank you.'

I move closer and plant a kiss on his stubbled cheek before leaving the kitchen and returning to the study.

Sliding into the black leather office chair, my jeans rub against the material and it makes an unnatural sound, like a polystyrene cup being crushed in a fist. Somehow, the noise is fitting. Comfort is void, and in its place a sensation in the pit of my stomach. I'm not normally superstitious; I don't believe in God and the concept of fate terrifies me, so external forces generally don't play a part in influencing how I feel. But today, now, I feel on edge, (*like an alert animal?*) all senses heightened, knowing something big is coming.

Trying to shake the dread, I spin slowly round in the chair and survey my chaotic office. I've been writing for as long as I can remember. The shelves to my left are a mess of paper work and books with folded over corners. My well-used leather bound Thesaurus has seen better days. I found it in a second-hand bookshop. For some reason, I have always preferred the feel of a book to the Internet or Word to find alternative suggestions. The silk thin paper between my fingers is comforting. I'm not great at moving with the times. Begrudgingly, I started to write using my laptop, and what pained me most was that it was brilliant. The speed at which I could get the words down, the Autocorrect, all helped make life easier. But I still can't get to grips with a Kindle. I want a book in my hands, with paper pages I can turn and a smooth colourful cover I can stroke with the palm of my hand.

Charlie calls me a dinosaur. He's right, the irony being in the fact that I make my living selling eBooks. As of yet, none of the big boy print publishers have taken me on.

I'm told the problem I have is that none of my stories fall into clear genre categories – as though that's a bad thing. But I shouldn't complain, I am one of the lucky few. I get to do what I love and a small percentage of people buy my books. We are not rich. We couldn't be, on a small-fry writer's earnings and the salary, Charlie gets as a recruitment agency manager, but we are comfortable enough and privileged to own our own house, with the help of a mortgage.

I sit back in my chair and stare out of the small window onto the dark street. Our Victorian terraced house on Shipton Street is small but perfectly formed. We have a good sized eat-in kitchen, a cosy sitting room with a log-burning stove and a small extra room downstairs that serves perfectly as my office. Upstairs is the bathroom, our bedroom, which has a pretty iron fireplace as does the spare room in which there is enough space for a single bed. At the back of the house is a small patio garden chock-a-block with pot plants, a bistro table and chairs.

My life was so much simpler before. Until now, I've been content wondering without needing to know. The mystery was enough but she's gone and shattered my serenity with a letter and repetitive bloody phone calls. I'm not ready yet, not ready to talk to her, to hear her voice.

I remove a cigarette from the pack on my desk and light it. Instantly, I feel calmer. Charlie pokes his head round the door and frowns. He hates that I smoke at all, and gets especially cross when I do it inside. So, I put my hands up and slink out of the chair, heading for the back door.

When I step outside, the freezing air makes me catch my breath. It is unusual even for February. The papers claim the country is in the grips of a mini ice age, but I think it's all tosh. The Middle East is temporarily calm and the US isn't dropping bombs on anyone. It figures they need to find something to write about. I wrap my beige poncho cardigan tightly around my front and smoke the cigarette quickly before returning to the heady warmth of our kitchen to find Charlie sitting at the table pouring over the Guardian. He recently had to admit he needed reading glasses. They sit awkwardly at the end of his nose, not quite at home yet. Still, to me he looks handsome and elegant. Looking up from the article, he smiles.

'Bed?' He folds his paper.

'You bet.' I fill two glasses of water.

'Things will look brighter in the morning,' Charlie turns the light out as we make our way towards the stairs, 'You'll see.'

I nod but my head throbs and in the pit of my stomach, I doubt he is right.

February 8th

I wake to find myself dripping in sweat. The fear lingers for a nasty moment before I sit up to find Charlie sleeping next to me, his mouth slightly ajar, a drop of dribble gathering in the corner of his lips, and I realise I am at home. Still, my heart thumps and it takes a moment before I can trust reality.

He is naked beneath the covers and I nuzzle into his armpit inhaling the musty male scent he produces in his sleep. I feel like a little girl – safe at last.

My hands search his sleeping body and eventually rest on his morning erection. He stirs in his sleep and I dance between wanting to wake him and allowing the moment to remain only mine. Then the feel of his warm, hard phallic compass rouses something in me and instinct takes over. My mouth slowly works its way south down his warm belly, passing a forest of wiry curls and the canyon of his belly button. But, moments before I make contact, he is awake and attempting to sit up in bed. And when this happens I rouse, as if from a Shakespearean dream, clouded in the shroud of a rich purple mystery.

Now, there are two of us sharing a place in this alternate universe, complicated and uncertain but as tempting as an intravenous drug with which we have dabbled but not fully succumbed. So, while I sit here, comfortable in the dirty sheets, it would be easy to make plans and pretend yesterday never happened. Visions are never what they seem.

While the winter has its blanket over this hard city and everything we know, hot thoughts bury themselves in the faded autumn and I find myself returning to earth with an unusually soft landing.

He sits up in bed and scratches his beard. Sleep gathers in the corner of his bright eyes and he yawns stretching out his arms like Christ on the cross. Sinking back into the pillows, he looks at me and cocks his head slightly to the left.

'You OK? You look a million miles away.' Reaching out his hand, he places it on the base of my back and strokes his thumb against my skin.

'Fine, just didn't sleep that well. You?'

'Like a log,' he says with satisfaction.

'Busy day at the office planned?' I try to shake the heavy sleep that pulls at my brain.

'Nothing major, a few meetings; the usual. How's the book coming along?'

'Slowly.' I say, begrudging the morning, sinking into the bed and pulling the crumpled, green duvet up around my body. 'I might stay in bed for a bit.' I close my eyes. For some reason I don't want to look at him this morning. I don't want to communicate.

'Want some breakfast in bed?' He slips out of bed and pulls on a pair of navy cotton boxer shorts.

'A cuppa would be lovely.' I pull the duvet over my head as he draws the curtains and lets the low morning sunshine flood our bedroom. From beneath the hot darkness, I hear as he leaves the room.

Charlie is my rock. As he walks to the bathroom, I hear him humming the Match of the Day theme, and it makes me happy. He can't sing, he can't even hum in tune and I'm not sure I could live without him. I feel so privileged that he loves me, too. Slowly, I pull back the duvet and sneak a look at the morning. From behind a naked silver birch, the sky is a cloudless, powder blue. I wonder what the day ahead has in store as I hear the boiler kick into action that means Charlie has turned on the shower.

On my cluttered bedside table, the clock reads 8.19 a.m. and I know I should get up. Then I spot the letter slipped in between the pages of the novel I'm reading. Gingerly, I remove it and unfold the crisp white paper. The address is at the top.

It took a few weeks but I did finally respond. I wrote a short, even curt, letter, giving my phone number. It had felt necessary to respond with something. My letter had gone in the post on a Wednesday and by the Friday evening, the call had come. I am glad to say, I had popped out to get a bottle of wine and Charlie had answered the phone. The moment I got back, he told me. I have avoided answering the phone ever since.

I've read this letter so many times over the past weeks and still find it confusing. What does it mean "an olive branch"? We didn't fall out for Christ' sake. My brain begins to thump and I rub my temples before putting the letter back inside the book and shoving it into a drawer. Out of sight is out of mind, I tell myself, knowing that is not the case. I can't deal with all these questions at this hour. First things first - coffee and toast - then perhaps I'll be able to think more clearly.

I slip my feet out from beneath the covers and the icy air numbs my toes as my feet make contact with the cold pine floorboards that creak with age. Pulling a powder pink towelling robe from a hook on the back on the door, I wrap it around my semi-naked body and head down the narrow stair case and into the living room where I turn the television on and allow the dialogue of a BBC news presenter to fill the house.

This is my morning routine and it never differs. Next, I turn on the kettle and put two slices of brown bread into the old toaster, which always tries to burn my breakfast, no matter how low the setting.

Above me, I hear Charlie padding about in our room. I can almost feel him dropping his damp towel on the floor and leaving it there for me to tidy later. I inwardly smile. It's the things only *you* know about the other person that make it so intimate and private. The same way I know he has left his towel on the floor, I also know that he will leave his dirty plate, egg cup and used mug in the sink instead of putting them in the dishwasher. But I don't mind. I really quite like cleaning up after him, the same way I enjoy cooking the evening meals. In turn, he goes to work everyday, to a job he hates, so that I can have the career I want. This is a real marriage. It may not be exciting, but it is comfortable and familiar, like a favourite old jumper.

Sitting down at the table, I manage to spill some of my coffee onto my piece of honey toast and curse. Nothing worse than soggy toast. Ripping off the bit that is beyond salvation, I hurl the damp bread across the small kitchen and into the sink, congratulating myself on my aim and accuracy. Then, I feel eyes on me and turn. Charlie standing in the doorway, frowning. I squirm in my chair like a little girl who has been discovered with her hand in the cookie jar and his face melts.

'You're a bloody slob,' he says sipping from my steaming mug, 'but I love you.'

He plants a kiss on the top of my head and strokes my bed hair before grabbing his battered old messenger bag and heading for the door.

'Have a good day.' I call with a mouth full of food as I hear the front door close.

February 9th

After a morning spent working on the story about a mother searching for her kidnapped daughter, I decide to take myself out to get lunch.

Grabbing my keys from a hook near the door, my grey wool coat, black wool scarf and bucket bag, I step out onto the street. In the distance, I hear a police siren. I pull the collar up around my neck. It's bitterly cold despite the gentle sunshine, and I walk quickly along the pavement listening to the sound of my green converse high tops connecting with the ground. Heading south, I make my way towards Bethnal Green Road all the while trying to concentrate on the plot of my book and trying to push away intrusive thoughts that hang over me like a rain cloud.

When I reach the bustling centre of Bethnal Green I'm greeted by the sight of its colourful street market. If you need cheap luggage, knock-off cleaning products, clothing, scarves or miscellaneous junk, this is the place to come. Women wearing thick winter coats over their sari's, wander up and down the road chatting to one another in Arabic, while the men smoke furiously and make business deals on their mobile phones.

I love East London. Here, micro-systems rub along happily, like bacteria under a microscope, multiplying. One moment, you are walking through Turkey, then you turn a corner to find yourself in Israel, while on the other side of the road, the rich live their decadent lives, paying through the nose for their organic vegetables and mineral water sourced direct from melting icecaps, turning a jaundiced eye to the existence of the great unwashed.

Something is always going on. Arty types wander the streets in the latest vintage gear, sporting glasses they don't need in order to see, and drinking overpriced cocktails out of chipped teacups. Exotic food smells waft from up-market restaurants, small cafes and busy takeaways. You can get anything you fancy at any time of day, from Vietnamese or Ruben sandwiches to Halal Kebabs or Caribbean. No other place in Britain has such diversity. It inspires me with awe that so many different types manage to co-exist in such limited space. Yet, amongst the hustle and bustle it is easy to remain anonymous. That's why I love it. You can lose yourself here. People don't notice one another - Some dislike it for that reason, but it's why I've made it my home. If you aren't sure you belong, then this is the place for you. In this limitless, unpredictable city, I met Charlie four years ago.

Having got my degree in English at Bristol Uni, I stayed in the city for a few years where, as a waitress, I jumped from bar to bar. Then I found my feet in my favourite and longest lasting job working in a large bookshop.

But, friends gradually drifted away, most to London. I finally decided to follow them, waved goodbye to Bristol and moved to a shared flat in with another girl I knew and one other, I didn't. Another few jobs waitressing, I then managed to get a job working as a PA for a city banker.

I was hopeless as a PA and after three months of muddling my boss's appointments and forgetting basic tasks, I was out on my ear. I didn't even feel uncomfortable when David Philips called me into his large shiny office to tell me I was a waste of space and an embarrassment to his company. He was the kind of young, revoltingly unattractive, fat cat you see in the movies. He wore expensive suits that did nothing to hide his short, podgy figure. His hair was thinning around the temples and mousey, glued to his scull with enough wax to concrete a car park. Despite his vast pay packet and eye-popping bonuses, the man had as much class and style as a doughnut. So, when he read me the riot act, I was only to happy to tell him where he could stick his job, before turning on my high heels and tottering out of his office. It was one of my proudest moments.

I'd packed up my desk and was on my way home, carrying a small, pathetic box of things - a ropey pot plant, a few pens, a hairbrush, a packet of biscuits and some stationery.

I still hadn't quite got to grips with wearing heels on a daily basis, and managed to trip over a protruding flagstone and drop my box of belongings. A man passing by stopped to help me pick up my things.

I was not in the best mood and picking up on this, he asked me if I was all right.

'Not really, no,' I said. 'I've just lost my job, broken the heel on my shoe and laddered my tights. And it's not even lunch time yet.' I was unnecessarily aggressive while trying to scrape the spilt soil back into the pot.

'Not the best start to your day then?' There was a glimmer in his eye.

Until then, I hadn't really looked at him. He was a tall man with a thick head of dark hair, striking brown eyes that shone in a broad face. He carried a cool about him, like Harrison Ford crossed with Joaquin Phoenix. He wore a pale pink shirt, navy linen trousers with brown brogues. I noticed his large, gentle hands as he passed me my beloved Parker pen.

'Thanks.' I was thawing.

'No problem.' He stood up and dusted off his trousers. 'I was just on my way to get a coffee. Fancy joining me?' The question was delivered casually, but I could tell he was nervous.

Without a second's hesitation, I said,

'Why not? It isn't as though I have anything else to do.'

There was one of those bins attached to a lamppost nearby, into which went the broken plant, shoes, and having pulled off the torn tights, them, too.

Barefoot in the street, wearing a black pencil skirt and a cream silk blouse, I smiled at him.

'Let's go.'

That was the beginning and I've never looked back.

Four months after that propitious meeting, I moved in with Charlie. He was the first person who encouraged me to pursue my writing. He said one of us should follow our aspirations and that he was happy to support us both financially, while I tried to get my career off the ground.

A year later, we bought our own little house and got engaged. I was thirty-three. The wedding was a small, intimate affair, the service held in Camden Town Hall followed by a boozy lunch in Soho. It was the best day of my life.

Weaving in and out of people, I make my way to Macdonald's. I failed at being vegetarian long ago and my guilty pleasure is now having a Big Mac for lunch once a month. As I step into the restaurant today, I look forward to the food more than usual. That smell of chips and gherkins fills my nose and I queue behind an obese black lady and her two small children, one of who is also far too fat and picks his nose with disinterest while staring at me, blank-faced.

Eventually, I reach the checkout. My order is taken by a spotty Asian youth with greasy black hair and long gangly limbs. He's so shy he's unable to look me in the eye as he hands me my change and while I wait for him to fetch my burger and chips. The kid slides the brown tray over to me and looks over my shoulder at the customer behind me, a Polish man covered in paint-spattered overalls who is talking loudly on his phone. Moving out of his way, I spot an abandoned table near the large window and make a beeline for it, taking a seat where I can look out onto the pavement and passers-by.

I take off my coat, unfold the waxy paper and reveal a steaming sesame seed bun overflowing with lettuce, meat, onions and sauce. The food smells hot and sweet and picking up the burger with both hands, I sink my teeth in, tearing off a large bite. Sauce drips down my chin and spills out onto my fingers. I reach for a napkin and wipe my face and hands before noticing my reflection in the glass opposite. My auburn hair looks messy and is hanging just below my chin. Maybe, I should get it trimmed before...

I notice a spot of food in the corner of my slim pale mouth and quickly wipe it away with a thin, rough paper napkin before removing a few chips from the red box and shoving them lazily into my mouth. The salt coating is a welcome introduction to my taste buds. Then I return to staring at myself. I wonder what she looks like; a fellow redhead with hazel eyes and freckles across her nose? Probably not, but you never know. Is she pretty, plain, or quirky looking? The questions buzz around my head in sync with the noise from the ice cream machine in the background.

I finish my fast food fast and leave. I'm in a rush to get home. I've come to a decision and I want to put my plans into action before I change my mind. My heart thumps in my chest as I hurry along the cold pavement, winding my way through the back streets, determined. When I get home, I'll call her. I will take my coat off, hang up my keys and bag and then I will be brave, pick up the phone and dial the number.

I arrive at the house, and unlocking the door, I notice my hands are trembling. I stretch out my fingers and watch them quiver. Stop it, I tell myself. I go inside. The house is warm. The hands are still shaking. It's not the temperature that's affecting me. I shrug my coat off, throw it over the bottom of the bannisters, dash upstairs and grab the letter. I run down again to my office, stand by the telephone, and, hands still shaky, re-read it for the hundredth time.

I wish it wasn't typed. Her handwriting would offer more insight into the kind of person she is. I scan the words looking for clues and questions somersault around my head. *Why wait so long to get in touch? What does she want from me? What is she like? What is her surname? Is she married?*

I dial the phone number in the letter I realise I am holding my breath as I count the number of rings. *Three.... Four... Five...*

'Hello?'

I freeze. Is that her voice?

'Hello,' she says again.

Still, I can't speak.

'Hello?' she says again, this time with frustration. I snap out of it and manage to respond.

'Hello.'

I don't know what to say.

'Hello, how can I help you?' *Is it her?*

'I'm... can I speak to Aileen, please?'

There is a brief silence.

'Can I ask who's calling, please?' The voice sounds suspicious.

'Is Ailene there, please?' I dodge the question. Another silence and then,

'Speaking.'

With that one word my stomach knots and a wave of nausea works its way up my body.

'Hi,' I speak quietly, 'It's Josie.'

'Hello, Josie.' Her voice sounds clipped. I hope she's as nervous as I am. There is yet another silence, only this time it seems to last much longer. 'I been hoping you'd call. You got my letter, I assume?'

'Yes.'

With my left hand, I am fiddling with a biro, twirling it in my fingers, continuously clicking the end.

'I don't really know what happens now.' The burst of honesty surprises me.

'Neither do I,' she sounds taken back, slightly defensive. Good, I think to myself.

'What would you like to happen?' Ailene is regaining composure.

'Honestly, I don't know.'

I lean back in my chair and slowly spin myself round. There is a low creak.

'Look, I am really sorry about this but it's not exactly a good time at the moment. I've got a lot on.'

I can barely believe my ears.

'Can I call you back another time?'

'Sure. Whatever suits.' My words are cool.

'OK. Good.' In the background, I hear a raspy coughing. 'I'll call soon.'

'Speak then.' And I hang up before she has a chance to respond. I feel rejected all over again.

I go over to my desk, remove the letter that has been taunting me for the last few weeks and go through it yet again. Was there something I missed? That I failed to comprehend? I look for any hint that might help explain her change of direction. *She* wrote to *me*, not the other way around ... but I don't find it ...

Flat 2,
Rigdale House,
Derwent Drive,
Bletchley,
Milton Keynes
MK3 7FS

Dear Josie,

After hearing from the adoption agency I've been
informed you are happy to allow me to write to you.

I don't know where to begin. We are strangers yet I
carried you inside me for nine months – it's strange.

There are reasons I couldn't keep you. I was young, only seventeen when I fell pregnant. In those days, it was different. I have a lot I would like to say but feel it would be better to do it over the phone or in person.

It must have been a shock when the agency called and told you I wanted to get in touch after all this time.

As I grow older I realise I have made mistakes in my
life and would like an opportunity to put them right.
I hope for a chance to explain why I decided you would be better off with an adopted family.

This must be a confusing time for you and by no means do I wish to pressure you into seeing me. I appreciate it will take time before you reach that point. But for now, know I have extended an olive branch.

Should you decide to contact me you can write or if you would rather then you're welcome to call me at home. My number is 07234 112869.

I hope to hear from you soon,

Best wishes,
Ailene.

She gave me up, and I kind of understand it. Thirty-six years ago, teenage pregnancy was not unheard of but attitudes towards it were far less forgiving. It might have ruined her life had she opted to keep me. I'm not bitter and I'm not angry, but I am puzzled.

February 21st

I wake up with a splitting headache. Jesus, this hangover is bad. The air in our bedroom smells of stale breath and booze. I sit up and the room spins as my feet find their way into my grubby stripped slipper boots. I realise I am still in the clothes I was wearing yesterday. Shame hits me like a bullet and I rub my temples hoping to erase the fog. On my bedside table is an untouched glass of water. I reach for it and down the tepid contents in one go. My mouth is so dry and I'm gripped by an unquenchable thirst.

I don't know who I am.

Am I drunk?

Am I high?

Looking down, my hands look like they belong to someone else and my head feels foreign.

All I know for certain is that I am self-indulgent. That is real. Anyone who has ever known me will confirm that. But I'm not as bad as my Mum. I'm not referring to the woman who brought me up, who nurtured me, loved me and wanted me. I'm talking about the woman who carried me in her womb.

It all stems from her, I tell myself. Also, that after all these years, things are different. They're not. I'm still me and questions still linger over my existence like a poisonous fog.

So much has happened in my life in the last week.

My life emulates a cruel experiment and I feel trapped in a Petri dish.

There is no recollection of going to bed. Did I see Charlie last night? Looking at the clock. I see it's nearly eleven a.m.. Damn, I trip over a jumper lying on the floor before kicking it violently out of the way. There is enough to contend with today, without my clothes trying to obstruct me. The fluffy orange jumper joins a pile of dirty washing in a far corner of the room. I know damn well the pile will remain there until Friday when I decide to tidy before the weekend so that Charlie doesn't think I sit around all day doing nothing.

Turning away from the mess on the bedroom floor, I decide I need to clean my teeth. Running my tongue over my front teeth, I know I neglected to brush them last night and, once in the bathroom, I see where my lips meet there is a dark reddish brown stain leftover from the glasses of Rioja. Guilt and self-pity mingle together in my head as I spit a large mouthful of white foam out into the basin below. I am dreading the day ahead. Drinking doesn't suit me, the hangovers are crippling.

In a bowl full of random crap, I find a hair band and scrape my untidy red mop off of my face. Beneath my eyes are dark bags reminding me of my own silly mistake. I splash some icy cold water onto my face and dry it roughly with a towel in the hope I might feel better. I don't.

Downstairs, I see the evidence of last night's excess. On the kitchen table sit two empty bottles of red wine, leftover Indian takeaway and the crumpled letter from my mother. The room smells of lamb Biryani and I gag. It seemed like such a good idea last night. Before I allow myself a coffee, I start to tidy my mess. The place looks like a student house. The yellow rice has gone hard and dried to the plate and I have to chip away at it over the kitchen bin before plunging the plate into a steaming hot sink full of Fairy bubbles. I put the empty bottles in a plastic bag and notice there are red rings of wine on the table. I scrub hard and eventually they fade.

The room looks respectable again and only now do I reward myself with breakfast. I make an extra strong pot of filter coffee and pop two pieces of brown bread into the toaster. My head continues to thump and I get myself a large glass of water. The pressure in my skull is unbearable, as if screws are being forced into it from all angles.

As I munch the warm toast, I start to feel drunk again. The food hitting my stomach is stirring up the alcohol and I feel it work its way through my system, flooding through my veins making the world feel distant again. I like the numbness. It helps me forget. Then the phone rings and wakes me from my daze. The sound is piercing and offends my tender ears. Gingerly I answer.

'Hello?'

'You're awake then.' Charlie sounds cross.

'Oh don't be like that. I feel shit as it is.'

'So you should. I'm not bloody surprised, the amount you put away last night.' There is a silence and then, 'Did it help?' He knows the answer. 'Jo, I get it. I really do. You're hurting. But delving into a bottle isn't the answer. I don't recognise you some of the time.'

'I know,' I am frustrated by the truth. 'How's work?'

'It's a pain in the arse. The phone hasn't stopped ringing and Michael is on my back.'

Michael, Charlie's boss, is a huge hunk of a man who spends hours in the gym when he's not "closing deals" or "shagging birds". He's a fifty year old who looks like he's in his thirties, due to his African skin. I've only met him once but I was struck by the cheapness of his shiny grey suit and mauve coloured tie. The faux diamond stud in his ear clinched the deal. It's fair to say I think he's a prick.

'I want to the kill the sod.'

In the background, I hear a phone ringing in Charlie's office.

'Jo, I have to go. Sorry. I'll call again at lunch. Love you.'

And before I've had a chance to respond, the phone line goes dead. For a while, I remain looking at the phone in my hand. I feel painfully alone. I'm reminded of my childhood. I grew up in the country and lived a privileged life. Yet, the one thing I really wanted was a real family, one I belonged to.

Fiona and Harold Griffin adopted me when I was a tiny baby. She was a wonderful mother. The softest, most gentle woman I have ever known and so unlike me in every way. It must have been difficult for her when I was growing up. We are so different. She is calm, ordered and chic. I am a chaotic redhead with a temper to match. It must have been disappointing to discover she didn't get the little darling she'd no doubt hoped for. None the less, she never showed it. She always told me she loved me and was proud of me and I am grateful for the effort she went to.

The thing I remember most vividly about her was her hair. Long, blonde and poker straight, it would gleam in the sunlight like the surface of a lake. I thought she was a princess when I was little.

As I grew up, we grew apart. Then, when I went off to university, the space between us grew wider. I saw them less and less and only spoke to Mum on the phone once every couple of weeks. Standing, holding the phone in my hand, I wonder if I should call her now. Would it make me feel better to hear her voice? The answer is no. I put the phone down on the table and decide the only thing to do is go back up to bed.

March 13th

This has got to be the dullest place on earth. The wet concrete roads slitherin' through the countryside are never endin'. The grass fields go on and on and the only thing to break the monotony is a few trees or a wild hedgerow.

It would have been impossible to make a note of the route; thank fuck for GPS.

The damp scent of bark is all around me. I will have to wash my clothes when I get home.

Funny what you think about when you are alone, in the woods, at nightfall. I never knew there could be so many shades of brown. Shiny brown, dull mustard brown, dog shit brown; fifty shades of crap. But, you know, I'm really very happy here, slitherin' in the wet mud bidin' my time.

To hunt an animal, you have to put yourself in their shoes. Crawlin' through the dark, damp woodland floor, I know I'm doin' the right thing.

My senses are heightened and I feel an electric current permeate the air around this place.

Just as I beginnin' to think I am makin' some progress, there is a flash in the sky. A beam of light cuts through the trees and I freeze, droppin' to the ground. Lyin' perfectly still, I wait for a long time before the sight and sound have been disappeared for some time.

I'm certain the car didn't see me, but although I am hidden in the undergrowth, and the darkness blankets, me I will remain cautious.

It's best to remain invisible for now.

And then as if on queue, the rain begins again. It is relentless and before too long I know the elements will win.

But I remind myself, my mission is important. I made a promise to her and I won't fail.

As if some celestial body has heard my plea, the rain parts and I see a fallen oak tree. The dark hollow space beneath is dry, warm and invitin'. This is the place I am meant to be.

Crawlin' with my arms and knees pushin' down into the soggy ground, I count the seconds it takes to reach the cold, cavernous space. Its trunk is so thick. I feel invisible.

My black jeans are heavy, caked in mud and leaves and my trainers feel like concrete slabs tied to my feet. My only blessin' is that I'm wearin' a polyester jacket and the slinky fabric glides through the filth in which I wallow.

Restin' face down, my breath clouds in my face offerin' me welcome moments of warmth and the adrenaline that rushes around my body finds a home in my groin.

Rolling over, I find myself lookin' through the naked branches at the indigo night sky. It's not romantic. There are no stars. But it is peaceful and the universe assures me that nothin' will get in my way.

I'm reminded of the fragility of time as I check my watch. The black plastic Casio tells me it's seven twenty p.m. Time drags and I curse. How long must I wait? The promise of what's to come reawakens a stirrin' in me and I grip the bulge in my trousers, enjoyin' the feelin' of heat spreadin' through me.

My mind is plunged into a spirallin' world of sadistic lust I had temporarily put on hold.

Fumblin' in my rucksack, I remove some of the items and lay them out on the hard ground. First comes a bottle of water, then a torch and finally a porn mag. Some things I deemed vital to this job. For now, I don't require the water or torch. It is the images that will get me through. The smooth skin, black leather, lace and stretched arseholes will keep me company.

As I stroke my shaft through my trousers, I look into the eyes of the brunette who is staring back at me. Her large swollen tits burst out of her bra. A small scrap of nylon pretends to cover her pussy. But the best bit is her lip-gloss. Her mouth is so shiny, she looks like she's just sucked dick. And the more I think of this, the harder my stroke becomes until at last a warm explosion of fluid erupts from my cock and starts to trickle down my hand. The warm, wet, stickiness makes me feel more alive than I could have imagined.

But just as I really start to relax, I hear the crack of a twig in the distance and suddenly all of my senses are reawakened.

Lyin' perfectly still, my dick going flaccid, I wait until I'm sure it's safe to move. Just a dumb animal I tell myself as I begin to peel myself off the ground and repack my bag before checkin' my wristwatch again. 9.48 p.m. Not long now.

I slip the rucksack over my shoulders and crawl in the direction of the house.

Remember, this is all for her. It's what she wants. My mantra keeps me goin' as the cold begins to get a hold of me again.

Then, at last, like a lighthouse in the distance, I spot it. And it is magnificent. A large, detached late Tudor house, with land and views to die for. I instantly hate the inhabitants and look forward to causin' them pain.

The house is built of stone with a cross-gable roof. It is roughly a horseshoe shape with a more modern extension extendin' to the eastern side. All that I know is learnt. My research has been extensive. But, without lookin' into the past, it wouldn't be easy to access the type of people who lived here and inhabit this prehistoric relic.

From where I lie, in the dirt, I'm still able to see it for what it is - a palace of lies.

I see a paddock in the distance and imagine a lonely horse grazin' in the moonlight. I know the history of this place. A little girl, alone, hopin' for the world and bein' given a pony.

'Be quiet.' The voice said. 'They won't believe you. You'll be sent away again.' And a broad hand ran its chubby fingers down the child's cheek. 'Shhhsh. Shssh.' His whiskey breath made the eight-year-old want to wretch but she never moved a muscle. Instead they lay still and didn't breathe a word ...

Without knowin' it had happened, I suddenly found myself in an open field, surround by a ragin' wind and covered in blood.

I couldn't remember how I'd arrived there and it took some moments before I realized where I was.

My hands were wet and warm and slippery. I no longer felt the cold. Calmness kept me in a cocoon.

It was only when I entered the house, my hand strugglin' to grip the door handle that I realized I was covered in thick blood.

I'd gone to the stable and killed his fuckin' horse with a pitchfork. Over and over, I plunged it into the animal's neck.

Within half a second, the smell of iron and cells had taken hold of my senses. It was a kind of blood lust that was animal, archaic, primal. It would have been pointless for me to try to resist.

I couldn't tell you how I made it up the stairs. I really don't remember. It was just one of those things that happened; One minute I was outside slaughterin' the animal, the next I'd got inside.

My erection was vicious, unrelentin' and I thanked the Devil I'd been given this opportunity. Not many men were this privileged and very few would ever be able to say they lived like I had.

Crawlin' on my hands and knees, leavin' a trail of the blood, I eventually found my way to the master bedroom. My hands shook with sexual anticipation when I realized I'd made it. I looked down at the latex gloves and took a deep breath. The smell of blood on my clothes was intoxicatin'.

The house was as quiet as a tomb and I listened outside the door for signs of life. There was none.

I relished how easy it had been. A vein in my temple throbbed and reminded me how frail life was. My stiffy grew harder still and it was all I could do to stop myself from masturbatin' on their landin'. But after a few long, deep, breaths, I managed to regain my composure. I had a job to do, I told myself, as I slipped the bag quietly off my shoulders.

Until then, I had left one section of my bag unzipped. But now the time was drawin' near, my quiverin' hand edged towards the zip and suddenly I could smell the semen again, like chlorine and stale sweat minglin' together. But the feel of the cold, hard metal brought me back to where I was and gently I removed the crowbar from its compartment.

Nothin' had ever weighed so heavy in my hand and I didn't miss the significance. If anythin', it makes the experience stronger. Better.

With no warnin', I found myself landed back in reality. No longer was I on the landin' caressin' the crow bar. I was leanin' over the old man shakin' with anticipation.

She laid next to him, in the bed, a knife stickin' out of her chest and wide, shocked, eyes starin' lifeless up at the ceilin'.

She never saw it comin', but I'd make sure his agony would last.

With one confident hit, I split his skull. The sound was like a tyre poppin' or an egg fallin' to the floor. But that wasn't the most shockin' thing. What really took me back was the look in the old bastard's eyes when he heard his head shatterin'.

His expression was hopeless and somehow disappointin'.

It didn't last long enough.

He was dead before I could really enjoy his agony.

For some time, I remained still, looking at him. Numb.

Then I did the only thing I could think of. I bashed his face in.

Bits of brain and bone exploded into the air in a beautiful display of reds and pinks. Temporarily, my world lit up and all the things inside of me had a voice, a violent, bloody meanin'.

Then I removed the bottle of bleach from my rucksack and drenched the fuckers in it.

The next thing I remember is walkin' back along the main road; a ghost dressed in black. Just another lonely person on a country walk, a man with no destination.

The day is beginnin' to break and I recognize the weight of my existence. My hands ache with violence and my throat is soar from suckin' in other souls' last breaths. My shoulders feel heavy and I remember my rucksack. There are a few precious things.

A soggy porn mag.
A gold Rolex watch.
One bloody crowbar.
Bone.

The weight of the body part suddenly hits me.

What am I carryin'?

But then my shoulders relax and a grin spreads across my face like a fire. A piece of his broken skull. She would be pleased, I remind myself as I slide through the mornin' back towards the land of the intangible.

I am safe in the knowledge that no one will see me leave.

They never have.

March 14th

The sound of my own laboured breathing wakes me. I look around through clouded vision and try to focus on the world.

Where am I?

Then instinct kicks in and I sit up, pushing the hot stuffy covers back off of my sweaty frame. It feels like the bars of a prison have been lifted. My body feels lighter, freer somehow.

Scrabbling about, my hand finds an abandoned glass of water on the table next to me. This can't just be coincidence.

My mouth is thick with fog and I don't recognise the smells that surround me.

A slender, pale arm comes into view. A scattering of freckles sprinkled with fine arm hair standing to attention. It looks foreign and I examine the silver and turquoise bangles that jingle around my wrist. There is only one word that springs to mind – "Boho".

I sit up and rub my eyes; the world around me starts to feel familiar. On a pine chest of drawers on the right side of the room, I spot a photograph of two people embracing. The image is backlit by sunlight pouring over the couple.

Then I see his face from behind the 6" x 4" glass, and at last the penny drops.

Charlie. Charlie, there you are. I thought I'd lost you.

And as if by magic, the bedroom door swings open and he appears, carrying a tray laid with scrambled eggs, brown toast and a large mug of steaming hot tea. Smiling, I slide back down the bed.

Balancing the tray on my thighs, he carefully sits down on the edge of the bed.

'Miss me?' he says and I'm reminded of an orphaned puppy.

'Like a hole in the head.' I keep my eyes closed and picture him naked.

Before I know it, he's removed the tray and is pulling the duvet down, revealing my body.

'Missed this?' He allows his tongue to slide down my tummy towards my knickers.

Part of me wants to fight him and part of me longs to succumb. A battle rages internally as chemicals and hormones dance around my system beating their drum.

But, before I have a moment to think, he has spun me onto my front and is grazing my shoulder with his teeth. I feel a prod against my buttock and then he is in me and I am shuddering with each thrust.

'Fuck you. I'm going to fuck you.' Although the words come from him, they sound alien and before my climax is in sight, he has finished.

Lying on top of me, like a spent whale, I thank Destiny for what she has delivered. This is love. This might not be what people dream of but it's real. No hollow fairy tales here.

I want to touch myself and start it all up again, but I can't. He is too heavy lying on my back, pinning me down. But the thrill is still there and I struggle to abandon it without a fight. Something has taken over. I feel alive and fired up.

He rolls over onto his side of the bed, his cock tired.

'How's my girl?' `he asks, eyes closed, a small smile across his face.

'I don't really know.'

The statement lingers and I wonder if I even said it. My head feels thick and I sink back into my pillow scrunching my eyes shut determined not to let the world in.

Then his hand searches me out like a mole underground and I feel instantly better. His touch changes everything.

'I'm sorry we fought.' I roll over and face him.

'What?'

I don't understand his confusion.

'Don't make me say it again. I'm going to stop drinking so much, OK?'

'OK, Jo.' His lack of animation bothers me suddenly.

'What time is the game on?' I say, stroking his face.

'Which game?' A frown creeps across his face.

'The United game. What time are we playing them?'

Charlie sits up suddenly and rubs the back of his neck with his hand.

'That was yesterday. We watched it on Match of the Day. Remember?'

No. I don't remember.

'Oh yes, but I meant, what was the score? I kept falling asleep and I'm not sure I know the final result.' I hear myself tripping over the words and feel ludicrous.

'Fucking draw.' He says and wrinkles his nose. 'We should have won. Sturridge was on fire and they were lousy.'

Why does none of this resonate? My head throbs.

We lie in silence for some time and I listen to the soothing sound of his breathing. I can tell from the hum that he is almost sleeping and his relaxed demeanour starts to rub off on me.

With a loud sigh, I move into his body and wrap my arm around his waist. His penis is still on display and I can't resist moving my hand over the shaft and giving a gentle squeeze, to which, he smiles.

'Got enough energy for round two?' I whisper into his ear, enjoying the feel of my warm breath.

Silently, he turns onto his side, facing me, and lets his hand find my crotch. His fingers briefly dance in my pubic hair before searching for a point of entry.

With his thumb, he stimulates me. I bite down on my lip and push my pelvis towards him.

The rest of the day we spend flopping about. I live in my slippers and he doesn't get out of his blue towelling dressing gown. The television is on in the background while he lies dozing on the couch. In my office, I try to write something new but struggle to put words down. My head isn't in the right place. I haven't written anything for days and days.

Bringing my knees up to my chin, I hug my legs. There is a faint smell of sex on my skin and I inhale, enjoying the memory.

Then out of the corner of my eye, I see my calendar handing on the wall. The uniform squares separating the dates are a mess of red and black ink, arrows and circles where I've made plans, changed them and changed them back. But the thing that stands out to me is my father's birthday. In a week, he will turn seventy-four. I'm reminded of the mess my relationship with my family is in. My stomach does a flip and I push my office chair away from the desk before spinning round in it and jumping out.

Charlie is still on the sofa, an arm thrown over his face, one testicle hanging out of his robe, and as I sit down carefully beside him, I think he is all the family I need. But then a thought cross my mind like a firework lighting up the sky. What if two became three?

I hadn't considered children with Charlie. We'd met, moved in and married so quickly, there had barely been time to make other plans. But now, sitting in our cosy London home, it all falls into place. I know he is older than I but that shouldn't matter. Without question, he would be a wonderful father. Doubts hang over my ability to parent but one thing is clear, I couldn't do a worse job than my mother. I would never abandon my child.

So excited by the prospect, I wriggle on top of Charlie and start to kiss his face. He grunts and tries to turn over but there isn't enough room on the sofa. He grunts again.

'Jo...' he grumbles, 'just a few minutes peace.'

'No time for that, lover.' I nibbled his ear with just a little more vigour than usual.

'Oow.' He pulls his head away suddenly alert. 'That hurt.'

'I just want you to wake up.' I say in my best little girl voice. He opens one eye and looks at me.

'Yes?'

'I want us to have baby.'

I say it as if I've requested pizza for dinner. Both eyes now open, he sits up to face me.

'Are you serious?' He appears bemused.

'Deadly.' I say fixing him with a smile. He cocks his head to one side and folds his arms across his chest.

'You've never mentioned it before.'

'It hasn't been something I've thought of until now.' It is my turn to cross my arms now, mirroring him. 'I suppose in the back of my mind I just thought it would happen one day and there was no need to mention it.'

Charlie nods but says nothing.

'You aren't exactly getting any younger and I'm a good age, so yes, why not now?'

I don't know if I'm trying to convince him or myself. He inches closer to me on the sofa and puts his arm around my shoulders before kissing my hair.

'Absolutely.' He says and I am stunned. 'But make me a promise. No pressure. Let's not try too hard. Let nature take its course.'

'OK,' I say, pushing him onto his back, 'but practice makes perfect.'

March 16th

Only a day has passed since we decided to try to get pregnant and, although I'm sure nothing has happened yet, I feel like a new woman. I've stopped taking the pill and keep finding my hand resting on my belly. I'm already mentally planning how I'll rearrange the house when we need to make space for our baby, and all the things that will come with it.

This new excitement has even meant I've started to write again. Life feels good and I've been able to shake off the discomfort of Ailene's advent into my life.

I haven't spoken to her since I called the first time. There's no point. If she wants to talk, she knows where I am. She made contact first, for fuck sake. That's what really gets my goat. She came into my life uninvited and then just as I started to get my head around it, she dismissed me.

Standing in the kitchen, I physically stop and promise myself I won't get wound up. I have a new exciting chapter just around the corner and nothing is going to spoil it. Not the hale outside, the war in Syria, the extremist terror threat hanging over Europe like a cloud – none of it is going to impact on my happiness.

I put the plates away in the cupboard and wipe my hands dry on a grubby tea towel. I fling it over the back of a chair before leaving the room.

Today is a good day and I am going shopping.

I think about leaving the house. There has been a break in the weather. The pavement is no longer pelted with hailstones. A grey sky blankets London reflecting the concrete streets. I look to the sky through the window, examining it with curiosity. Is snow in the air? It is so white, so clean and full of promise.

In the background, I hear the hum of news. Normally the whining tones of the Sky newsreader float over me but today the sound is genuine and solemn. I can't ignore it.

Moving towards the voice, I feel my stomach flip.

'The plane was flying at thirty two thousand feet... an airbus A230 has crashed...fell for eight minutes... flights cancelled... no known survivors... a very sad time says President...'

And before I get a glimpse of wreckage on the screen, I decide to turn around and walk away.

All it takes is a minute to change how you feel.

Back in the kitchen, I stack more plates and sweep crumbs off the table onto the floor. The crumbs only remind me of the plane. That quick. Once it was a piece of toast now just crumbs discarded amongst the dust and debris that has collected on the tiles.

Surely, life is not so fickle?

I feel ill. I am consumed by the thought that I'm dying. I catch my breath and as quickly as the thought enters my brain it is gone, distracted by the infinite ringing of the house phone.

I move towards the sound. Each step is more psychedelic than the next and I wonder if I am on the flight, falling, crumbling away.

Somewhere in the distance, I hear a dog barking.

Then I flood back into the moment and remember the phone.

Holding my breath, I manage a whisper.

'Hello…' The taste of bile fills my mouth and the silence emphasises it. 'Hello?' I ask again, my throat on fire.

Nothing.

'H-E-L-L-O?' My last attempt.

Nothing.

But then I think I hear something distant. A whisper. Muffled.

I wait again, holding my breath.

Then the line goes dead.

Just before I collapse onto the carpet, white noise echoes down the line.

I wake up to find my face buried in the living room carpet. My neck aches and my arm, which is tucked awkwardly beneath my body, is numb.

Slowly I sit up. The ceiling and walls feel as if they are closing in and I look around the room that feels foreign to me. For a few seconds, I am lost but then I notice a photograph on the wall. I see Charlie and I on our wedding day and I'm brought back to earth.

Gingerly, getting up onto my wobbly legs, I make my way towards the picture hoping to find comfort. It helps to calm me but I am scared. What is happening to me? I keep losing time. How long was I passed out on the carpet? My mouth tastes of metal and I realise I've bitten the inside of my cheek. Blood and saliva gather in the corners of my mouth and I wipe it away with the back of my sleeve, trying to focus my attention on Charlie's face.

For the first time ever, I notice the age gap between us. He looks happy and handsome, but old. His face is creased while mine is pale and fresh. It doesn't bother me, but it feels as if I've woken up in an unfamiliar world.

What was I doing before I collapsed?

Moving over to the couch, I flop down into the cushions and look up at the ceiling. A wispy cobweb dangles from the ceiling being blown by a draft from an unknown source. I really must try harder at housekeeping.

A cold shiver runs through my body starting at the top of my head and working its way down to my toes. The small hairs on my arms point north and I shake myself warm. This is ridiculous. I need to get a grip.

I get up, still feeling a little like Bambi and decide I need to see a doctor. Something is wrong with me and I need to get to the bottom of it.

Just as I reach for the phone, it begins to ring and a strange sensation falls over me. Remembering the cold caller, I answer warily.

'Hello?'

'Hello. Can I speak to Josie please?' The voice sounds shaky.

'Speaking.' I say trying to place the familiar female.

'Oh, oh Josie. Gosh, I didn't recognise you...' There is a long pause. I rack my brains trying to place the voice.

'Margaret?' I take a punt.

'Oh Josie, I...' It is Margaret. Her voice is breaking and all of a sudden, I feel faint. Something bad has happened. I sit down on the sofa.

'What is it?' I swallow down the lump in my throat.

'It's your parents, Sweetheart.... You need to come home.'

'What's happened?'

'I...' She stops again. There is another voice in the background talking to Margaret. I can't make out the words. 'You need to come home, love.'

'Tell me what's happened. Mum, Dad, are they alright?'

'The police are here.' She offers as an explanation. I am none the wiser.

'*The police*? Why?'

'Your parents, oh I don't know how to say it. They, I'm so terribly sorry but... they are dead.' Her thick Gloucestershire accent has faded to a whisper.

I hold the phone to my ear. She must be mistaken.

'Josie, love, you need to come back.'

'What do you mean? I don't understand.'

'I went there this morning to clean and when I got there. Oh Josie, it was awful. I called the police and now they are everywhere. I saw, people carrying a body out of the house. I didn't know who it was. Then this detective came over and questioned me. He said there had been a break in and two bodies had been discovered in the house...'

I feel strangely calm as she tells me her story.

'... I told them the only people who live in the house are your parents. They asked me if I had any contact details for the next of kin. I came home and gave them your address. They are on their way to you, now. I... I shouldn't have said anything. They told me not to but I didn't want you hearing it from a stranger. Josie, it's just terrible. I am so sorry.'

'Did you see them?' I am running on autopilot.

'Who?'

'The bodies. Did you see their bodies?'

'No. Goodness no. They were in bags.' The thought turns my blood cold.

'So, you didn't see Mum and Dad?'

'No, but ...'

'So, it might not be them.' I interrupt.

'Josie, well I ...' She doesn't know what to say.

'It might not be them.'

'Josie, they said it was a couple, found in the master bedroom,'

'But it might not be them.' I repeat. There is a long silence.

'The police are on their way to you now, love. I think you need to talk to them.'

'OK, Margaret. I was going to go shopping but I think I should wait for them.' My words sound as absent as they feel.

'Yes, I think that's a good idea.'

'OK, yes, I'll wait here.'

'Alright, love. Are you on your own?'

'Charlie is at work.' My words come on autopilot.

'I think you should call him. Tell him what's happened. You shouldn't be alone,'

'He's got meetings.'

'Call him, Josie.'

'OK.' Another long silence follows.

'I am so sorry.' She says at last. 'You have my number. If there is anything I can do…'

'I'll be fine.' I pick a piece of fluff off my knee and watch it float down to the carpet.

'Call Charlie, love. Promise me?'

'Yes. I will. See you soon. Bye.' I hang up and stare at the piece of grey fluff on the carpet for a long time and wonder where it came from. It looks like cat hair.

I decide the room could do with a good hoover. Moving with purpose, I go into the hall and pull our old Hoover out from a cupboard under the stairs but my mind is somewhere else. It has left my body.

I plug in the Hoover, start to suck up the dirt, dust and fluff that life produces, hardly noticing the roar the machine makes. I work hard pushing the head backwards and forwards over the same spot until I'm convinced it's clean. I should do this more often, I scold myself, before I succumb to a sudden wave of exhaustion. My legs feel frail and sweat drips down my temples. I sit down on the floor, my legs crossed. I notice my hands are trembling, like they do sometimes. Of course, my hands are trembling. *My parents are dead.*

Without really knowing I'm doing it, I reach for the phone and dial Charlie's work number. His mobile will be set to silent. There are three rings before someone answers. It's a young woman's voice.

'I need to speak to Charlie.'

'May I ask who's calling?'

'His wife.'

'One moment please...' Gentle jazz plays while I hold. The noise is as irritating as a fly.

'I'm afraid he's in a meeting at the moment. Would you like to leave a message?'

'Tell him to call me at home. It's urgent.'

'Right, OK,'

I hang up before she has a chance to finish and remain sitting on the carpet next to the discarded Hoover. My hand is gripping the phone, willing it to ring. I stare at it, frozen in time. The numbers on the buttons are all swirling into a blur. I am finally brought back to earth with the ringing.

Answering the phone, I wonder what I'd say to anyone who wasn't Charlie. *Sorry can't speak now; my parents have been killed.*

'Hello?'

'Jo, hi. Is everything all right? I got an urgent message to call.'

'I had a call from Margaret. She said the police are on their way. I don't think I can do this alone. Please come home.'

'Who's Margaret? What are you talking about?'

'Mum and Dad's cleaner. She said there was a break in.' A lump returns to my throat. 'They found two bodies at the house. It might be Mum and Dad.'

There is a long silence and I wonder if I'm imagining the phone call.

'I'm coming right back. Don't do anything. Sit down and wait till I get home.' His voice sounds distant. 'Jo?'

'I think my parents are dead.'

The next few hours go by in a flash. At some point, Charlie returns home. Then the police arrive. The next thing I know I'm sitting in the back of a car being driven to Gloucestershire. The traffic is sluggish and the March sky a bleak grey. Charlie holds my hand the whole time, occasionally giving it a squeeze. I don't respond.

I notice darkness is starting to fall. Glancing at the clock in the car, I see it's nearly half past five. The car comes to a halt in front of the large concrete police station. The police officer that drove us turns the keys and the engine dies. None of us make a move to get out. I feel Charlie's eyes burning into the side of my face but can't bring myself to look at him. His sympathy is too much to bear.

Unsure what to expect, I push open the passenger door. The cold wind is the first thing that hits me. Looking down at my feet, I realise I am still in my slippers and feel foolish.

A young policewoman hurries by, offering a small friendly smile as she passes. Her kindness hits me like a slap in the face and I lean against the car for support. Charlie appears at my side and slips his arm through mine.

'You can do this. I am with you.' The warmth from his body soothes me.

The detective who drove us here gestures for us to go inside. But before I am ready to move, I need some answers.

'What is going to happen?'

'I suggest we go and sit down. I have a few more questions. Then…' He looks at the floor

'You want me to look at the bodies, don't you?' I ask meeting his eye.

'I'm afraid so. Yes. But that won't be until later tomorrow. There needs to be a post mortem first.'

'I want to see now.' I tell the detective.

'We need time to prepare.' He leaves the sentence unfinished.

'I am not going to answer any questions until I know it's them.' The detective and Charlie share a look, shocked by my determination.

'Come on love, let's at least go in and have a cup of tea first. Give yourself some time to prepare.'

'How can I ever be prepared for this?' I swing round to look at him. 'Either it's them or there has been some huge misunderstanding. I need to know before we talk anymore.' The detective steps closer to me and I notice for the first time how lanky he is.

The darkness is deeper now, looming overhead a charcoal sky and indigo clouds gather and I half expect the four horsemen of the apocalypse to appear galloping through the sky, breaking through the clouds.

'I understand, but I am afraid there is a procedure to follow. We cannot risk contaminating any evidence. The earliest you will be able to view them is tomorrow. I suggest you come in and have that cup of tea.'

March 17th

It's just after midnight. At the police station, I drink tea from a polystyrene cup. It's nearly too hot to hold but the uncomfortable heat is soothing somehow. The room is small and brightly lit. A blanket that Charlie requested sits on my shoulders but still I feel shivery. Every time the fabric brushes against my skin, it feels itchy. I wonder how many criminals and victims have been wrapped in it before me.

My hands tremble as I grip the cup. I suppose I am suffering from shock. Numbness keeps me in a bubble, unable to cry, unable to feel anything.

We are waiting for the detective to return. He has some questions. He is not the only one. I wonder how I can help. I wasn't there. I didn't see anything. This is all so surreal.

'Where the fuck is he?' Charlie wriggles in his seat. He's never been very patient.

I put the cup down and fold my arms on the table in front of me, slumping my head down.

'I'm tired.' It's all I can manage.

'Right, that's it.' He stands up puffing out his chest.

'Leave it.'

'No, they can't keep you in here. This is ludicrous.' He starts pacing around the table. Watching him doing laps makes me sick with dizziness.

'Please Charlie,'

'This is totally out of line…'

'Please,'

'Either they come now or I'm taking you home and they can wait...'

'Shut up! Shut the fuck up!' I blurt out as rage surges around my system. Charlie comes to a sudden halt. He looks at me as if I am a stranger and I bury my face in my hands.

'I can't do this. Not now.' I feel the tears well up. 'I don't need you to fight for me. Just, please, just sit down.'

'Ssshhh.' Charlie moves closer and pulls up a chair.

'Just sit with me, please.' My voice wobbles as my throat closes up and I feel the blood drain from my face. 'I think I'm going to be sick...'

Retching, all I manage to bring up is the tea. My stomach is empty since I had no lunch. I have no idea what time it is but decide it must be late as I wipe my mouth with the back of my hand. On the lino floor, a small puddle of frothy tea pools at my feet.

'I'll get something to clear it up.'

Charlie leaves the room pulling the door closed quietly behind him just as my body begins to shake uncontrollably. I have lost all control of my muscles and slump onto the floor convulsing as gradually the walls around me close in and everything turns black.

When I regain consciousness, a smiling, Asian face greets me. The blanket that was around my shoulders is now tucked under my head. It smells of cheap washing powder. Behind the brown face, I can make out Charlie's silhouette, dark and looming, similar to my nightmares – a faceless threat.

I feel like I'm drifting through the sky in an air balloon. The oxygen is thin and my chest is tightening. I'm scared. Waiting to fall, expecting to crash into the hard, cold ground. But this is not *me*. It is someone else. I am behind a mask living someone else's life. A fraud.

That is how I feel as I come to.

Instantly, the drama of the situation wraps its arms around me and I feel the grip tighten.

The halogen lights in the station hurt my eyes and the role I am expected to play bears down over me with crushing weight.

Wake up.

Wake up.

My eyes open and I fix on Charlie.

He is here, so encouraging.

'I think she's waking up,' someone says, the words bringing me back into the present as I carefully sit up.

'You OK, love?' Charlie steps forward. I don't respond. 'Get her some water,' he barks at the young, kind faced policeman who has stepped back. 'Let's get you onto a chair.' His attention is focused on me once again and I nod in agreement, as he lifts me carefully from the ground and guides me towards a blue plastic chair. 'Sit.' It is as though he is speaking to someone with dementia, but I do as I'm told.

Once safely seated, the room of unfamiliar faces begins to clear until the only people who are left are Charlie and I.

'You gave me a bloody fright.' He says, bent down on his haunches.

'Sorry.'

'I'm going to take you home. This isn't right. Not being here now. We can come back tomorrow if they want but I'm getting you out of here.'

'We can't go back to London,' I prompt, 'I need to be here.'

'Fine, then we'll check into a hotel.' He is always the practical one. 'I'm going to speak to that detective. Just sit here, all right? Don't move. I'll be back in a flash.' He takes my hand, kisses it and places it back in my lap before he struts out of the room, an intent figure.

I am left alone in the soulless interview room and I have a sudden urge to run. All I want is to get up out of the hard chair and run as fast as I can away from the police and the horror inside my head. No more reality. I've had enough to last for one day. My brain wages a battle - accept reality or deny it.

A noise snaps me out of it as the young Indian policeman comes through the door, carrying a glass of water. His deep brown eyes smile with sympathy as he places the cup on the table.

'You should drink this.' He rubs his neck with the palm of his hand. Looking up at him, I realise how young he is, probably only in his early twenties...

'Thanks.' I pick up the glass and take a sip of water. It feels good. Then I turn back to the officer. 'Is this your first murder?' I am genuinely curious. He fidgets on the spot and nods nervously. I didn't mean to spook him and realise he thinks I am judging him. That was not my intention. In order to put him at ease, I say the first thing that comes to mind. 'Mine, too.'

March 18th

'It's alright to be scared.' Charlie reaches out a hand and rests it on my shoulder.

'I just want this over and done with.' I feel like shrugging him off but resist the urge to push him away. This is not his fault. I stand up and tell him I need the loo, an excuse to put some distance between our bodies.

'I'll be right here,' he says as I dash out of the room.

Finding myself in the vast corridor, I feel lost. I don't belong here. The morgue is a grim, sober place. I realise I don't know where the loo is, so just stand in the corridor for a while, taking some deep breaths.

Can I smell blood?

Then someone appears from one of the rooms wearing forensic overalls and takes a step towards me.

'I just want to go to the loo.' I sound pathetic. Before the man can reply, I hear a familiar voice behind me and spin around to find the detective.

'We are ready for you now, Madam.' His hands are grasped together and I notice his knuckles are bony and white. 'This way please.'

Charlie appears from the waiting room. I've never seen him look so solemn. I can guess how he feels. His heart has always ruled his head.

I know how I should feel. But I can't get there. I'm not even scared. Not really, although I know I should be. I'm waiting for it. No doubt it will come. It'll grab me by the throat and choke me until I wake up and realise this is actually happening.

As we make our way towards the room where my parents are, I realise a nightmare would be easier. I could wake up and comfort myself that it never really happened, that it was just my twisted imagination going for a wander. But that is not the case. I am really here, each step taking me closer to the two bodies that lie in wait.

Will I see blood? Will their eyes be open? Is it them?

I've never seen a dead body before. Mixed with fear is a lingering fascination.

As we reach the door, I feel Charlie's hand on my shoulder.

'I am going in by myself.' I say and he releases his grip, stepping back. The detective, whose name I struggle to remember, pushes the white door open and beckons me in.

Inside, the room is luminous white and I feel exposed by the bright lighting that prevent any shadow.

Looking to my right, I see a figure in robes standing next to two tables that have bodies laid out on them. The pair lay covered in white sheets so I cannot see their faces but already I know it is *them*.

My father is unmistakable. Even concealed, the size and figure are unmistakable. My blood run colds as I remember him living. He is, *was*, a great hulk of a man with a large belly and double chin. Portly, some would call it, but in truth, he was plain fat.

My dry eyes turn to look at the veiled body of the woman. Tall, slender, neat. Just as she was.

The pathologist clears his throat and our eyes meet. I nod and he moves over to the male body first, carefully peeling back the sheet. But he doesn't show me his head. Just the body. The head remains covered.

'There was too much trauma to the skull.' He speaks in a muted tone. I try not to imagine what is hidden beneath the sheet.

Dad.

Then, silently, the next figure is revealed. This time, I see the face.

Mum.

I stare at the corpses. She looks the same as she once did, but somehow different. I can't put my finger on it. Without realising it, I move closer to my mother.

The coroner steps closer and tells me not to touch anything.

Then it hits me. Her hair. They have styled it all wrong. She would hate being seen like this.

'It's them,' my feet are carrying me backwards towards the exit. 'It's my parents.'

April 12th

The next few weeks drip by and I survive it all on autopilot. Faithful Charlie remains by my side, helping me sort through all the endless piles of paperwork that accompany death.

We stay near the house I grew up in. My parents' were so proud of the place. Even at the B&B, I see ghosts round every corner and sometimes think I hear footsteps in the night.

The police have assigned me a counsellor, who tells me this is normal. She's a large woman with kind blue eyes that sit roundly in her pudgy face. I've only seen her a handful of times but the only thing I can ever concentrate on is that she smells strongly of instant coffee. It's as though the scent is coming from her clothes.

My best friend, Sophie, has been wonderful. She calls everyday to see how I'm coping. She's a high-powered prosecution lawyer in the city, so she has a greater interest in the case than most. Last time we spoke, I asked her to take her law cap off, as I need friends now, not legal advice.

We met at school when we were thirteen. She got to know my parents well. Sometimes, she came to stay during the holidays. Her parents are also well off. You had to be to go to our school. Rich was a prerequisite; clever was not. But Sophie was smart and she was going to do well at whatever school she was sent to. Meeting her was the best thing that came from being there.

I used to hate them for sending me to a single sex school. I was a tomboy who liked riding my pony, Foxy, and climbing trees. I missed Foxy so much when I was away. That was the worse thing about being at boarding school. It all seems so long ago now.

Detective Woolfson, (I've finally remembered his name) is in regular contact. He is a strange man, shy and uncomfortable around people. I'm told they are doing everything they can to find the people/person responsible but as the days pass, it is looking less likely. They appear to have no leads, have found no helpful clues and no evident motive. Robbery gone wrong is suggested to me, but I can't help thinking that the brutal nature of it makes it something else. It feels more personal than the police are admitting. But I just can't think why anyone would want to kill my parents. No one has any reason.

I've been told that the killer slaughtered my father's horse before breaking the glass in the back door and letting himself in. He then went upstairs and attacked my parents. There was nothing stolen except my father's gold Rolex. It seems strange to me that was the only thing taken.

Woolfson has explained that there were no finger-prints and that they couldn't find any trace of DNA on the bodies as the person responsible had used bleach to cover their tracks. It seems the assailant had then disappeared into thin air.

As I push that thought to the back of my mind, I'm reminded of the strangeness of my situation; just as one parent comes back into my life, two disappear. I wonder whether somehow there is a link and feel as if I'm looking at the pieces of a puzzle, unable to put them together.

Sitting in a chintzy armchair with my feet tucked up under me, I gaze into the licking flames of the small gas fire. Outside a cold wind blows and the branch of a tree scratches at the window. I am alone in the room with only my thoughts. I wish Charlie would hurry up and come back with the food. He left ten minutes ago to collect a Chinese takeaway from a nearby restaurant and already I miss him. I'm calmer when I know he is near.

Looking around the bedroom we've called home for the last few weeks only exacerbates my feeling of being lost. The furnishings and wallpapers are so far from what I like and am comfortable with. I feel like a stranger in my own life. The pile of clothes on the floor near the unmade bed helps me to remember, though. I am a chaotic, creative, confused orphan.

The sound of the door opening makes me jump and I swivel round to see Charlie dripping wet, holding a brown paper bag. The scent of five-spice fills the room and my mouth salivates as I hop out of the chair and rush over to him and throw my arms around his damp neck.

'Christ, I wasn't gone that long, was I?' He feigns strangulation.

'No,' jabbing him in the ribs, 'but I'm glad you're back. What did you get?'

'What didn't I get!'?

He shakes raindrops from his greying hair and slips his coat off.

'We've got duck and pancakes, prawn toast, spring rolls, beef with black bean sauce, seaweed, dumplings, Singapore noodles and prawn crackers.' He smiles like a Cheshire cat, proudly displaying a mouse it caught.

'Good work.' I start peeling off the cardboard lids of the foil containers, enjoying the hot steam that rises up and hits my face.

'Damn,' Charlie reaches over and picks up a spring roll, 'we haven't got a knife and fork.'

'Balls.' I have never been any good with chopsticks.

'I'll go down and ask if we can borrow one.' He heads for the door.

'So good to me.' I blow him a kiss and take a hot dumpling out of the box with my fingers.

Seconds after he has left and I have finished sinking my teeth into the dumpling, my mobile vibrates in my pocket. Irritated, I pull it out and focus on the screen. My mother is calling. But she can't be because she is dead. And then my brain makes the leap and I realise it is Ailene. Unsure whether or not I have a desire to speak to her, I slide my finger across the screen without thinking.

'Hello.' I'm aware that this reluctance is strange and guilt hits me like a punch to the face.

'Can I speak to Josie?' Her voice is clipped.

'Speaking.'

'It's Ailene.'

I know that already and wait for something more concrete, but the break in conversation seems to last forever.

'Hi.' I say eventually.

'How are you?'

How am I meant to answer that?

'I've been better. I'm dealing with some things at the moment,'

'Can I help?' she interrupts.

'Not really. Thanks though.' Another long pause leaves me cold.

What am I meant to say to her?

'I thought perhaps we might meet,' the suggestion hangs in the air mingling with the smell of Chinese food and I have the bizarre sense of déjà vu.

'Now isn't exactly a good time. I'm not in London. But I'd love to.'

'Where are you?' She is certainly direct.

'I'm staying near my parents.' The conversation feels stranger than ever now.

'Near Gloucester?'

'Yes.' I'm surprised she knows.

'I can come there.'

My brain starts to implode and I wonder if I'm imagining the conversation.

'I've got a lot on my plate at the moment, Ailene.' Her name feels alien. (I mentally note the similarity in the words) 'Please don't think I don't want to see you, I do. It's just...' I can't finish the sentence.

'I know about your parents.' She is so calm. 'I read about it in the paper. I am so sorry. I thought perhaps you might need some support.'

If it's support she is offering, why does she sound so glib?

'I'm sorry,' the panic rises in my throat, 'I can't do this right now.'

'Fine. That's fine. When you're back in London let me know and if you want I can visit.' She sounds cold again. I'm losing her.

'No, hang on.' The words rush out before I've had a chance to think. 'I'll come back to London. I need to get away from here. How about we meet on Thursday?' My hands shake.

'That sounds reasonable.' She could sound more enthusiastic.

'Come to my house. I'll make lunch.' I have no idea what day it is today.

'That sounds pleasant. I have your address.'

'Good. Well, I guess I'll see you then.'

'Indeed. See you then.'

'Great. Thanks. Bye.' I hang up before she has the chance to. Staring at the pile of food in front of me, I've lost my appetite.

Before I've had a chance to process the conversation, Charlie reappears brandishing cutlery.

'Got it.' He says proudly.

'I just spoke to Ailene.'

That kills his chirpy mood.

'Oh. How did it go?' he sits down on the corner of the bed.

'I'm having lunch with her on Thursday.'

'Oh. Good.' His apprehension is clear. 'Do you think now is the right time, love?'

'No I don't, but when is?' My head feels itchy and I scratch my scull ferociously.

'Fine.' He says picking at the Peking duck. 'I'll be there if you want me.'

'I'd love you to, but I need to do this on my own. I'm going stir-crazy in this place. This isn't *us*, we don't belong here. Time to go home.' He nods in agreement. 'Besides, the police aren't getting anywhere and you need to go back to work and I can't put my life on hold, waiting for them to make an arrest. We can't even bury them for fuck sake. I don't want to wait around anymore.'

He gets up from the bed, pads over to my chair and perches on the arm.

'Whatever you want, love.' He strokes my ginger hair.

'Take me home.' I bury my head into his jumper and close my eyes.

April 14th

Being back at home is strange. The last time I'd been there, I'd received the news of my parents' deaths. The house was just how we'd left it. Despite my frenzied hoovering, it was still untidy.

A begrudging Charlie returned to work. He wanted to stay and support me, but I was glad he went back. He was beginning to suffocate me. His well-meant kindness was starting to stifle me.

Charlie knew all about the relationship I had with my parents. He knew that I had hated my father and lost respect for my mother. But despite this, he expected me to mourn. I couldn't. I didn't feel anything. No sadness, no pity, not even a sense of freedom.

There was a great deal to do. I was their only child, so the aftermath of what to do with the entire property fell to me. But everything I did, I did out of obligation. I behaved the way I was expected to. I put my writing aside and dealt with the paperwork, bills, paying the staff that, apart from Margaret, included two part-time gardeners, a full-time cleaner, a groom who lived in a converted outbuilding near the stables. There was quite a bit to do on the practical side of things. For now, what would happen to the house could wait. The housekeeper Margaret, who lives in a small cottage that is part of the estate, would look after it.

I was going to inherit a fortune. They had done something right at least. The house alone was worth millions. Dad's classic car collection would make a nice nest egg, too. Charlie could retire. For the moment though,

I needed him out of the house. I needed time alone. Time to be numb.

I'm told we can't bury them yet and it's a huge relief. I couldn't face the idea of a funeral. Having to stand around and look solemn while all their bastard friends reminisce about what great people they were. Thankfully, that chore is on hold.

Now, I'm concentrating on the meeting. I want it to go without a hitch.

I've cleaned the house from top to toe, even going through the cupboards and throwing away old cans of food that we are never going to use. My nerves are on tenterhooks. It feels like my first day at a new school. My stomach churns with excitement and apprehension. Maybe, at last, I will find myself.

It's Thursday morning and I buzz around the house straightening everything. I don't know what food she likes, so I've filled the fridge with an assortment of options. If all else fails, there are pizzas in the freezer.

I keep checking my watch. It's 11.09 a.m. and the minutes feel like hours. 12.30 p.m. seems a lifetime away. Sitting at my desk, I browse the Internet to pass the time, looking at holiday destinations for when my inheritance comes in. Charlie and I always dreamed of going to Vietnam. He could take a sabbatical from work, or quit for good. The money I am due is going to change our lives dramatically and it feels like a new start is just around the corner. I thought I was happy. I think I was until a dirty crime changed everything. Perhaps moving would be a good thing. We could live anywhere in the world. But then I come back from the daydream and remember that I am about to connect with the woman who carried me in her womb. I'm not ready to walk away from that yet. I need to see how it goes. We may hate each other. I wonder how much is nature as opposed to nurture? Because another couple brought me up, does that mean she and I have nothing in common? I hope not.

Glancing at the clock again, I see forty minutes have passed and my stomach knots again with anticipation.

My phone beeps on the desk next to me. Fumbling with the buttons, praying she isn't texting to cancel our lunch, I open the message. It's from Charlie.

Are you OK? Xxx

I breathe a sigh of relief. Typing quickly on my screen, I respond.

Nervous as hell... Otherwise fine. Have a good morning. I'll call after she's gone. Love you xxx

Slipping the phone into my jeans pocket and turning my attention back to the computer screen, I realise I haven't written any fiction for some time. It's not surprising but the thought saddens me. Writer's block is a bitch.

I hope that once I've met Ailene and my parents are buried, I might be able to get back to doing what I love. It has been my happy place, my solace in the past and I miss the security that comes from getting lost in my own head, from making up characters and writing their stories. Writing is an addictive drug that gets under your skin.

Anna, a successful chick-lit author friend of mine, once asked me whether developing dark novels made me sad or scared for my characters. Understanding why she asked, I pondered for a moment before replying that I actually thrived on it. It just so happened, I tried to explain, that for whatever reasons, I liked writing about disturbed people and imagining events that might occur around them; that this interest made me feel alive and privileged, and not at all sad.

We went on to discuss how similar writing is to acting. The author must become his or her protagonist, must feel what they feel and think how they think. It is like having different personalities and giving a voice to each of them. One moment, you are a hero, the next you are a bitch. There is nothing better in the world than having the chance to live a thousand different lives.

I am lost in thought, plotting my next novel, when there is a knock at the door. The clock on the wall says 12.14 p.m., could it be her? I get up out of my chair and quickly check my reflection in the mirror, wiping away mascara that has smudged below my eyes. My annoying hands are trembling again. Walking towards the front door, famous words echo through my mind – *One small step for man, one giant leap for mankind ...* I know my thoughts are over-dramatic, but this is a huge moment for me.

On the other side of the door is the silhouette of a woman. The face is blurred through the glass and I can only see the outline. She is a similar height to me. At last, I know something concrete about my mother and this gives me the courage I need to open the door.

Our eyes meet and I see she is as nervous as I am. It makes me feel better. We stand there, looking at each other for a moment. She looks older than I thought she would. Her hair is cropped short, ginger traces remain but it is now salt and pepper at the roots and around her temples. She has a bony nose and a thin, pale mouth. Her eyes are almond shaped and dark brown. The skin around her neck is sagging. She wears no make up. She looks like the type that never does. Her clothes are modest and far from trendy. Beneath a black knee length mac, is a beige jumper, the type women in their eighties buy from Marks and Spencer. She has straight black trousers on and sensible brown boots. I don't know what I was expecting but the woman in front of me is not it.

She looks awkward. The silence between us has gone on too long. Feeling her tension, I back away from the door and gesture for her to come in. She nods and enters clutching a battered old silver handbag, a relic from the nineties that should not have survived.

It only takes a few seconds for me to form an opinion about her and I wonder what conclusions she has jumped to regarding me.

We linger in the hallway, a cold gust blowing into the house from the street. When I close the door, claustrophobia sets in.

'Please come through,' I lead the way into the sitting room.

Ailene stands near the window and I watch as she takes in her new environment.

'Can I get you a cup of tea? Or coffee?' My hands fumble with my sleeve.

'A glass of water, please.' Her voice sounds different in the flesh.

'Sure, no problem.' I dart into the kitchen leaving her standing uncomfortably.

As I run the tap, I have a moment to collect myself.

She is only human. Talk to her.

When I deliver the water, I find her sitting bolt upright on the edge of the sofa, still wearing her coat and holding her handbag on her lap.

'Thank you.' She takes the glass and has a small sip. 'That's better.' A small smile crosses her face. 'Would you like me to take my shoes off?' She bends to begin untying the laces.

'Oh no. No need.'

Sitting back up, I see that she doesn't approve and I feel foolish.

'How was the journey?' I can't think of anything else to say.

'It was fine, thank you.' She wriggles in her seat.

'Let me take your coat.' I approach with my hand out.

'Thank you.' She slips the mac off and hands it to me but keeps hold of her bag.

As I hang her coat up on a hook in the hallway, I take in the scent of fabric softener.

So, this is what she smells like...

I return to the sitting room and she awkwardly removes a small bunch of slight, tatty pink carnations from her handbag. She hands them over to me without saying a word.

'Thank you, they are lovely.' I take the flowers and sit down in an armchair opposite her. I know I should put them in water but I want to get down to business.

'So,' my heart is beating hard, 'you are my Mum.' The words sound strange.

'Yes, I am.' Her dark eyes do not waver but I look at my feet. 'I suspect you have a lot of questions. I'll do my best to answer but you might not like the truth.'

The statement shocks me. It is cold and unforgiving.

'I don't wish to judge. I just want to know where I came from.' I am apologetic.

'What do you want to know?'

'I suppose I want to know a bit about you. Your parents, where you grew up, that sort of thing.'

She is not making this easy.

'Well, I grew up near Liverpool. My parents owned a fish and chip shop in the town. My mum is still alive. Dad died a few years ago. My parents, John and Niamh are Irish Catholic. I have an older sister, Clara, and a younger brother, Fionn. I didn't do very well at school, partly because I fell pregnant with you. I stayed in Liverpool until I was eighteen. Then I moved to Milton Keynes. Never married, never had any other children. For the last twenty-five years I've worked in a haberdashery shop.'

'Oh, OK. Do you like sewing?'

Thirty-six years is crammed into a few sentences and I'm hit with disappointment.

'I do.'

This is like pulling teeth. Why did she bother coming?

'Do you sew?'

' Err, no. I've never been any good.' Again, a look of slight disappointment crosses her face. 'I'm a writer. I write novels for a living.'

'That's nice. What do you write about?'

'Thrillers, Horror, that sort of thing.'

'Oh. I don't read much,' *Great.* 'But when I do it's usually Danielle Steel. I don't like scary books.'

'Not everyone does.'

I'm sitting cross-legged in my favourite armchair talking to my birth mother and all I can think is that I could murder a vodka and tonic. This meeting is not going the way I hoped it would.

There is a long silence while we both try to come up with things to say. Fuck it, I think getting up out of my chair.

'I'm going to get a drink. Vodka tonic. Would you like one?'

'No, no thank you.' That look of disapproval flutters across her face again.

In the kitchen, out of sight, I take a moment to bury my face in my hands. I don't know which one of us is more disappointed.

Grabbing the vodka from the freezer, I take a quick swig from the bottle before making my drink and decide not to ask her what she would like for lunch. I am bound to get it wrong whatever I do, so I might as well just get on with it. I take a ready-made goats cheese tart out of the fridge and put it in the oven before returning to the sitting room. She is sitting in exactly the same position and hasn't moved an inch. Her back is straight. She doesn't slouch.

'Josie, that's a nice name.'

'Apparently my mother chose it because she loved little women. The main character is called Josephine, you know, Jo. Have you read it?'

'Not for some years.'

'Well, I never liked Josephine. I don't think it suits me, so when I was old enough, I decided I'd be Josie.' I wonder for a moment what name Ailene might have chosen. I look her dead in the eye deciding to take the bull by the horns. 'So, how was I conceived? What was my father like?'

She shifts in her seat.

'Well,' Ailene folds her hands together. 'I was very young. Seventeen, when I got pregnant. I was on holiday with my parents in Skegness. They had taken us in the caravan. We stayed on a site near the beach. It was a hot summer and lots of people had the same idea. The caravan park was very busy. Lots of families there with their children. I remember they had a disco every night. Everyone went.'

Remembering the past, she looks wistful, happy even. *This is promising.*

'I met him at the disco. He was on holiday with his parents. He was very handsome. He came from Oxford, I think. He was with his older sister and his brother. Anyway we got talking, we made friends and started spending time together. We'd go to the beach and eat ice cream. One night he stole some of his dad's beer and we went back to my caravan. Our parents were all at the disco. It was the first time I ever drank alcohol.'

I know what's coming next.

'He was very nice to me. I was drunk.' She looks so ashamed and I begin to soften. 'It was my first time.'

I nod and we sit silently for a moment.

'Did you ever see him again?'

'No, never. He has no idea you exist.' She is matter of fact and her brutally cold delivery leaves me breathless.

'When did you discover you were pregnant?' I regain my composure.

'We weren't very educated about such matters when I was young. My mother saw me getting dressed one day and took to me to the doctor. I was about five months gone. It was a horrible shock. I'd never been to bed with anyone before or after. It was only the once.'

Again, I am made to feel dirty.

'My parents were disgusted. They didn't want the shame of it. So, they sent me to stay with my aunt in Ireland to see out the rest of the pregnancy. There was no question I could keep you. The adoption was arranged before you were even born.' I can see sorrow in her eyes and I feel pity for her. 'They took you away minutes after I'd given birth. You were born on a Wednesday. That was the first and last time I ever saw you. Until now.'

'So I was born in Ireland?'

'Yes, in Dublin.'

'So, how did I end up living with a couple in Gloucestershire?'

'I don't know the details. It was arranged by my parents in Liverpool.'

The dinger on the cooker goes. The tart is ready.

'Oh, that's lunch. I hope you like goats cheese,' I call over my shoulder. As I slice the tart and prepare a salad, I process the information I've gained. *I have Irish roots. That explains the red hair.*

Dicing a tomato, I slip and slice my thumb open with the knife.

'Fuck,' I mutter to myself before sucking on the wound. The taste of blood makes me feel ill.

'You might need a plaster,' her voice makes me jump, 'shall I get you one?'

'No, no need. It's just a nick.'

She is standing behind me, as I turn on the tap, run my thumb under the water and watch the blood wash away down the sink.

'Please have a seat,' I gesture towards the kitchen table.

'It smells very nice.' She says taking a seat and putting the napkin across her lap. 'I like goat cheese.' I smile and a feeling of warmth rushes over me.

Perhaps this can work.

May 16th

I fuckin' hate public transport. The train smells of piss and all I can hear is a bunch of teenager girls sittin' behind me, talking about boys' dick sizes. I wonder what their parents would think if they could hear them? They've been talkin' about it ever since we left Euston Station. I'm sick to death of the sound of their voices but luckily, we should be arrivin' in Bletchley any minute and then I'll lose the bitches.

Lookin' out the window, I can see it's about to rain again, which is a pain in the arse. Now I've got to walk around in the soddin' rain, looking for the flat. I wonder what it will be like.

I've never been to Bletchley or Milton Keynes before. Always thought it was probably a shit-hole. As the train pulls into the station, I see I was right. The station is grey brick with a stupid metal roof that sticks up in the air. Although the rain has started to fall, I'm relieved to be away from those girls and all their talk. It gave me a hard-on listenin' to them and I didn't want anyone to see it. They shouldn't talk like that in public. It's not right.

As I walk through the station, I slip my hand into my pocket and take my phone out. I go to Google maps and type in the address I'm lookin' for. Derwent Drive.

After a few minutes' walk, I reach Rickley Lane. As I pass by, an old woman looks out of her shitty red brick house at me. I give her the finger and she drops the net curtain and disappears. Silly old bat. This is suburbia at its worst. I hate the place and all the people in it.

At the end of the street, I turn left on Whaddon Way. It is another road lined with red brick houses from the 1970's, just like the last.

Not far now.

My rucksack cuts into my shoulders and my boots start to feel heavy. I'm startin' to think I should lose some weight.

I pass a petrol station and stare at the people fillin' up their cars. A miserable lookin' lot, but then if I had to live in this place, I would be too.

It's funny how one day you don't even know a place exists and the next you are standin' there, in that place. I never heard of Bletchley until Ailene came into her life.

A few minutes later and I see the turnin' to Derwent Drive on my right. The rain is harder now and my heart sinks as I see it's just another road of ugly semi-detached houses. A few yards further on, I can see the block of flats. They're lower than I thought they would be, with only three levels. The walls are grey pebbledash and the roof, dirty red tiles. They look like a concentration camp. The kind of place little old ladies live who have no family. I suppose that's exactly what it's like, as I imagine Ailene comin' back from work to this buildin', her home.

I scoot around the back to take a closer look. It's not obvious which flat is hers but with the process of elimination, I work out she has to be on the ground floor. I'm grateful because that makes my job a whole lot easier.

Lookin' around me to make sure no one is about, I go up to one of the windows on the ground floor. I can see dirty plates in the sink and discarded takeaway pizza boxes and empty beer cans on the kitchen table. This is definitely not her place so I move on to the next window. The curtains are pulled but there is a gap enough for me to see a bed inside that has Spurs football sheets on it. Again, definitely not hers. I spit on the window and move on - Gunners all the way.

I move to the other end of the buildin' and start at the window there. It's a kitchen again but very different to the first. It's neat and tidy. There is a lace tablecloth on the table and a little vase of fake flowers sit in the middle. The sink is spotless and shinin'. Whoever lives here take pride in their surroundin's. On the wall, I can see a calendar hangin'. Upon closer inspection, I can see her handwritin' in the boxes. Bingo.

I go back to the front of the buildin' and approach the front door. It's got a security code lock on the door. I kick the ground and curse. Gettin' in isn't going to be so easy, after all.

The rain is comin' down hard now, peltin' the pavement with relentless force. Large puddles are formin' on the ground and my feet inside my boots are startin' to feel damp. Bloody weather.

But then a flash of a memory of bein' in Gloucestershire comes back to me, and I smile. Recollection of my vengeance gives me a rush and I feel a stirrin' in my groin. With the rain comes bloody violence – the place where I exist, in between the shadows.

It suddenly occurs to me that the rain might be my accomplice. The noise of the torrent could be enough to muffle the sound of breakin' glass.

I dash round to the back of the buildin' and after havin' a good look around, I push my elbow hard into the window crackin' it in several places. Then I remove my crowbar from my rucksack and push the glass in. It shatters all over the work surface in her kitchen. I hope she cuts herself when she has to clean it up. Puttin' on gloves, I reach in through the hole and open the window properly before jumpin' up and climbin' in.

The kitchen smells strongly of bleach, a bit like a hospital. Sterile. I move quickly, openin' all the drawers, rummagin' through the cupboards. In one cupboard, I find cans of food ordered neatly next to flour and pasta. The one next to it holds plain white plates and bowls. Casually, I take them out and let them drop on the floor, crackin'.

Next, I open the fridge and inspect what's inside. It's very bare. An iceberg lettuce sits lonely in the veg drawer. On the lower shelf is a box of eggs, a pint of milk and some cheese. The next shelf has a Tupperware box containin' somethin' that looks like cottage pie. I open it and taste a mouthful. The bitch can't cook. It needs salt. I empty the contents onto the floor and push it around with my foot. I need this break in to look like dumb kids, or fools on crack.

In the door of the fridge is a carton of orange juice. I take the lid off and drink the contents. It's cold and sweet and tastes good. Throwin' the empty carton onto the floor, I decide to go and explore the next room.

Her livin' room has as much personality as a wet flannel. Strangely enough, the smell reminds me of one. It's damp in here. The sofa is a small two-seater covered in brown Draylon fabric. The sort of thing a Nanna might have. It's ugly as fuck. An old fashion TV is in the corner of the room. It looks like it should be covered in dust but it isn't. I wipe my finger along the top to check.

The room is bare. The only decoration is a small vase of fake flowers in the netted window and a small wooden crucifix hangin' on the wall. No dust on that neither.

I go to the G-plan coffee table and pick up the sewin' left lying there. She's been doin' some embroidery. Lots of different colour threads are neatly lined up in a metal biscuit tin, along with various needles and pins. I study the picture she's started. It's cross-stitch, or somethin' like that.

A posy of flowers tied with a pink ribbon. It must have taken her a long time.

As I pick the stitchin' out and destroy her work, I can't help but smile. This woman is a sad, lonely bitch and lookin' around her house, I can see why. She needs to get herself a life.

Droppin' the ruined needlework on the floor I pull out my dick and piss all over it. My urine is very yellow and strong smellin', which is perfect. I enjoy watchin' the puddle spread and seep into the sludge green carpet. Getting' that out ain't goin' to be easy. That'll keep her busy.

After shakin' the final drops off the end, I put it away and wander into her bedroom. It looks like it belongs to a nun. There is a single bed, covered with a pink polyester bedspread, a small cupboard, matchin' chest of drawers and a little dressin' table. The person who lives here must be the dullest creature on the planet. I think about fingerin' through her clothes but can't be bothered. I'm so uninspired by my surroundin's. Instead, I lie down on the bed and look up at the ceilin'. It's got that bobble paint effect all over it and I start to see shapes in the plaster. Bein' in this place is like travellin' back to the 1970's and never findin' your way back. Reminds me of a prison.

Suddenly, I start to feel tired. I think it comes from disappointment. I feel empty bein' here. It's like lookin' at the reflection of a ghost. As I close my eyes, I remind myself I can't stop here. She could be back any minute. But before I leave, I have one partin' gift.

Rubbin' my hand over my groin, I stimulate myself. As I grow hard, I imagine that horse and remember the way it felt killin' those people. Rollin' onto my side, I pull out my erect, throbbin' dick and tug hard and fast. Just before I cum, I have time to get hold of her pillow with my free hand. I ejaculate all over it and finally wipe my nob on it. Then I get up off the bed, put the pillow back where it was, cum side down so she won't see it, and straighten the bedspread. It looks like I was never there and I smile at myself. The thought of her layin' her head down to sleep, restin' on my dead sperm, makes me chuckle.

I leave the room, pullin' the door closed behind me, and decide it's time to go. And just at that minute, I hear a loud bangin' comin' from the far wall. My heart quickens as I make my exit, back through the way I came.

Once outside, I pull up my hood over my head, coverin' as much of my face as possible, and disappear into a cluster of trees nearby.

I wait there till it's dark, before decidin' it's safe to leave and make my way back towards the train station.

May 18th

It's been a few days since I met Ailene. Our lunch went as well as could be expected, given the circumstances. We talked about getting together again soon before she left, which made me feel good. She said I should visit her and I agreed I would.

She was not what I was expecting. Nice as she was, I imagined someone a bit more out-going, maybe someone more like me. It crosses my mind that I am a bit disappointed, but I quickly dismiss the idea. Why should she be like me? We've lived such different lives. Besides, that was only our first meeting. She was bound to be tense. I certainly was.

Charlie was eager to get all the details when he got back from work and I told him everything I knew. His reaction was unexpected. He said he felt sorry for her. I hadn't thought of it like that until then. I suppose what happened to her was sad. She didn't really have a choice about what happened to her baby. I couldn't imagine being in her shoes at that age. Being a teenage girl is hard enough without discovering you are pregnant. I shudder at the thought, but then it gets me thinking.

I was having sex at her age. I had boyfriends. What would have happened if I had fallen pregnant? Would I have kept the baby? Would my adoptive parents have supported me? It's unlikely Mum would have been thrilled. Dad wouldn't have kicked up a fuss. I was his special little princess. But then I imagine having a baby living with me, in that house. With *him* there. The thought makes me feel sick and I push the bad memories away.

Not so long ago, Charlie suggested I sought counselling. He said that now they are dead, perhaps it's a good time to face my demons. I know he's right but now that they are gone, maybe I can bury the past with them. Dragging it all up again, with a stranger, seems like a waste of time. He's more help to me than any professional could be. I told him that and he seemed to accept it.

Yesterday, I slept all day. It was a dreamless sort of sleep that left me feeling as if I hadn't slept at all and I woke this morning feeling dog-tired again.

I'm alone at home today. It's another dull Tuesday morning. Charlie is at work and I'm meant to be writing. I can't manage it. An unseen force has imprisoned my imagination. There is a barrier in my head, blocking me from losing myself in the darkness I often call home.

I sit at my desk, surrounded by piles of paper, staring at the blank word document and swing in my office chair. It squeaks with age and the leather moans under my frame.

I'm so frustrated.

I avoid the bustling London streets that make my head hurt but our home feels small and claustrophobic. There is nowhere I can escape to. The murder of my parents hangs over me like a fog, even when I sleep. I wish the police could do more. They need to be laid to rest. The longer they lie in the morgue, the longer they will haunt me.

I check my watch. It's eleven thirty in the morning. All I've achieved today is dressing myself and eating a piece of toast. The house is in chaos as usual. No visitors today, so no need to worry. I don't know what to do with myself. The minutes tick by slowly while I wait for Charlie's return. He is working late this evening, which I hate.

There is only one thing for it. I go into the kitchen, open the fridge, which smells strongly of ripe cheese, and remove a bottle of rosé. I open it, close my eyes and drink straight from the bottle. It's cold and sweet and promises to numb me.

I take the bottle into the garden and sit on the bench, my knees tucked up beneath my chin, against the mild spring wind. The elements make me feel more alive, more akin to my surroundings. Outside, I can breathe again, and I watch my breath cloud in front of me like smoke.

Our small patio is coming into life at this time of year. The pots that have been empty vessels waiting the return of spring are alive again. A brown slug drags its fat body along the slabs, looking for nothing in particular. I wonder what it's like to be a slug.

When half the bottle has been drunk, I decide I crave the comfort of music and return indoors.

The warmth of the house hits me, wrapping its arms around my cold, skinny body. Slipping through the kitchen and into the living room, I go over to our old record player. The lid is dusty and I wipe the dead skin and hair away, leaving a grey film behind on my fingertips.

Sinking onto my knees, I run my hand along the spines of the LP's. I don't know what I'm looking for and I let my fingers do the searching. Finally, they rest on a red spine and I pull the album out. It's the Rolling Stones Greatest Hits. The cover features a large pair of open lips and a set of teeth, one of which is gold. I stare into the mouth and feel as if I am being swallowed up, before tearing my gaze away from the image, taking the large black disc from its sleeve, placing it on the turntable, carefully lifting the arm and dropping the needle into position. The room fills with the sound. I turn the volume up higher, determined to lose myself in the music.

Still on the ground, I remove my socks and let my bare feet feel the floor. The pine boards are cool and smooth below my pale white soles. I picture the floor once being trees, standing high and proud, leaves glistening under soft sunlight. I need to imagine them alive. There is too much death in my life.

Picking up the wine bottle and getting to my feet, I move over to the rug in the centre of the room, in front of the Victorian fireplace, and start to dance. I can feel the base rise up from the floor, and my body moves in time with it.

I start to feel better and swig more wine. After listening to a few songs, there appears to be a pause in the album. The tension builds in those few silent seconds and I prepare myself for what is about to come - *Paint it Black.*

As the last drop of the drink falls from the bottle into my open mouth, the music strikes up. Like an earthquake, it shakes the room and the pictures on the walls. Closing my eyes, my body becomes a snake, the music my guide. I am entranced and possessed by another being. It feels strangely wonderful. The looming darkness has dissolved along with my sobriety.

I wake up on the living room floor, clutching an empty wine bottle, a small puddle of dribble in the corner of my mouth. The phone is ringing and my head hurts. I push myself up off the ground with my arms and stretch my stiff neck. My knees crack as I finally stand and suddenly I feel old. The room spins as I search for the source of the ringing. Then I spot the phone, lying on the sofa and rush to answer. The movement makes me feel dizzy and I sink onto the sofa before pressing the button that will stop the dreaded noise drilling into my head.

'Hello' My voice sounds hoarse.

'Hello, it's ...'

There's a pause, but I know who it is.

'It's Ailene.'

'Oh, hi.' My head is pounding.

How long was I passed out on the floor for?

'I didn't really know who else to ring.'

She sounds troubled.

'What is it? What's happened?' A feeling of dread settles around me.

'I was burgled.'

'Shit. When?' It sounds awful but for some reason, I am relieved. It could have been worse.

'Yesterday.'

Suddenly she sounds clipped and I realised I shouldn't have sworn.

'That's terrible. Did they take much?'

'No, that's the strange thing. They broke in, made a mess then left. They didn't take anything.'

'Did they do much damage?'

'Nothing that can't be fixed. I called the police. They came out and said it was probably kids with nothing better to do.'

'It sounds as though the police were right. Are you alright?'

There is a long silence while she contemplates her answer.

'I was very shaken at first. Nothing like this has ever happened to me before.'

'It sounds horrid.'

'I feel so... so... violated.' There is a small crack in her voice. 'To think that someone has been in my home, looking through my things. It makes me feel so upset that someone could do that. May God forgive them.' Suddenly there is a tinge of Irish in her accent. 'I don't know what to do with myself. I don't feel very safe here.'

After our first meeting, I had wondered whether she was capable of showing any weakness. Now, I am grateful that she has.

'You can come and stay here.' I say without thinking.

'Well, I ...' the cogs in her mind are turning and I instantly regret extending the invitation.

'But, I'm sure you have somewhere else you'd rather go.'

'Not really.' She speaks quietly and sounds meek.

'Oh.' *Do I really want her to come and stay?* 'I mean, you're very welcome, I need to check with Charlie, but if you need a place...' Panic begins to set in.

'That's very kind of you.' Formality has returned to the conversation again. 'Speak to your husband and have a think about it. You have my number. You can call me later today, or tomorrow.'

I feel guilty at the thought of her having to spend another night alone in a place that frightens her.

'I'll speak to Charlie when he gets back after work, and then call you later tonight. Maybe you could get a late train?' *This feels too fast.*

'We'll see.'

'I'll call you later. OK?'

'As you wish.'

'And I'm so sorry about the break-in.'

'Thank you.'

There is a click and the line goes dead. I sit staring at the phone, trying to process what has just taken place. It seems as if the conversation happened to someone else, and I was on the periphery watching. Did I really just ask a virtual stranger to come and stay? Ailene is a stranger, after all. She gave birth to me and barely saw me. We have met once for a short, difficult time.

Shit. What have I done?

I sit back on the sofa and close my eyes. The world is still spinning and I can see faint shapes in the darkness. A sudden chill makes its way up my spine and I hug myself. Sitting there fretting isn't going to get me anywhere.

I go out into the hall and up the creaking narrow staircase to our bathroom. I open the mirrored doors of our glass medicine cabinet and search through the pills of boxes and bottles for some Aspirin. I need to think clearly and that means sobering up as quickly as possible. Swallowing a couple of tablets, I bring my face down to the sink and splash my brow with cold water from the tap. It's icy and does the job I want it to.

The next thing I need to do is to eat. As I tread each downward stair, I grow more aware of the cold and look down at my bare feet. It's bitter for this time of year.

I find the pair of thick socks I had been wearing, half sticking out from under an armchair in the living room. Slipping my feet into the grey wool has an instant, warming and sobering effect. I am no longer the crazy woman, drinking wine and dancing in bare feet.

Padding into the kitchen, I open the fridge door and for the second time that day, am hit by the stench of over-ripe cheese. I quickly close it again. No joy there. I move to the larder cupboard. There are tinned tomatoes, tuna, pasta, couscous, rice, flour, sauces and condiments, jars of spices, jams, cheese biscuits, dried lentils and chickpeas, but nothing takes my fancy. I want meat and it seems the only way I am going to get it is to venture out of the house.

In a bowl on the kitchen table, sit my keys and some money. I pocket both and head for the front door, pulling my coat off its hook before leaving the comfort of my prison.

I have finally made it through the rain to the Halal butcher on Bethnal Green Road, feeling cold, wet and pissed off. On the way, I was heckled by a laughing group of builders, taking a break from their work.

'Cheer up love, it might never happen.'

'It already has. My parents were just murdered.'

I stopped and scowled at them, enjoying watching the colour drain from their faces, and their eyes searching the wet tarmac.

Whether they believed me or not, who knows, but for a split second I made them stop. That feeling gave me something I've been lacking. It gave me control. This whole time I have felt helpless, but in that one small moment, I took command and it felt good. But, I am also irritated by the confrontation. Why is it that men think they can behave like that?

I shake the raindrops from my shoulders and the scent of flesh hits me at once. It is unlike anything else.

A grumpy-looking Asian looks at me across the counter, chewing his gum with disinterest. I seem to be offending a lot of people today. I approach the glass counter and walk slowly along it, gazing at the chunks of cut-up meat. No pork here. But I don't fancy pork. I stare at the whole chickens and think it might be nice to cook Charlie a roast, but in truth, I can't be bothered. All I can think of is myself, and what I want.

Then I spot it, sitting at the back. Red, moist beef.

I point to a large steak. The man reaches into the counter, with a gloved hand and removes the meat.

'One?' he has a thick accent, somewhere between Indian and East London.

'Just one.' I remove my wallet from my handbag, as he throws it down on the scales. He points at the price before wrapping it in paper and putting it into a small, white, plastic bag.

I pay and quickly leave the shop, holding the bag in my hand. The meat feels cold and solid in my palm. I put it in my pocket. I don't know why.

On my way home, I stop in another shop and pick up a lettuce, a bottle of red wine, a bag of frozen French fries and some chocolate. Happy with my choices, I make my way home, avoiding the route I took before and the bloody builders. It is the long way, but it doesn't matter because when I get home, I shall have steak.

On one of the small Victorian streets, my phone rings in my bag. I stop on the pavement, put my bag of shopping down and fumble to find it. It's Charlie.

'Hi, hi,'

'You sound a bit out of breath. Is everything OK?'

I press the phone between my ear and my shoulder; pick up the shopping with one hand, before taking hold of the phone again and starting to walk once more.

'Depends what you class as OK? So far today, I've had a hideous phone call with Ailene telling me she's had a break-in, and then some fucking builders on the way to the shop heckled me. Apart from that everything is dandy.'

There is a long silence.

'Is she alright?'

'Not really. Very shaken. Understandably.' My tone has softened and I remember that none of this is his fault. 'I'm sorry. It's just been a bit of a shitty day so far.'

'I don't know what you want me to say, love.'

'I just needed to vent.'

'You know I'd come home, if it was important,'

'No, that's not why I rang earlier. I've done something really stupid…'

'What is it?' Charlie sounds exhausted and guilt hits me on the face at the same time as a large raindrop falling from a leaf.

'I asked her if she wanted to come and stay.'

'Oh.' There is another long pause. 'Is she coming?'

'I don't know. I told her I'd check if it was OK with you.'

'Josie, love, if you want your mother to come and stay, you don't need to ask my permission.' Frustration is creeping into his voice and I feel my back stiffen.

'I know that. I felt sorry for her, and before I realised what I'd done, I'd asked if she wanted to come. Then I panicked. I thought maybe you might be able to offer some advise. I mean, I hardly know the woman.'

'Listen, if you want to ask her then go ahead, but honestly, I don't have time for this right now. I've got that prick breathing down my neck, a deal is on the brink of falling through and I'm tired. I'm really bloody knackered.'

'Right, well, I won't keep you any longer. See you later. Have a nice day.'

I click the phone off. I'm fuming. I'm so bloody angry. All I wanted was a bit of support.

Stomping through puddles, I replay the conversation and by the time I reach the house, I've calmed down.

It was unfair of me to put my troubles ahead of his. I didn't even ask him how his day was going. No wonder he was irritable. All the poor man has been doing over the past few months is listen to me go on about Ailene and my parents.

I get back to the house where the warm air embraces me. It is the hug I have been wanting, ever since I hung up on Charlie.

Cursing myself for being so selfish, I drop my shopping, remove my mobile and send him a text.

I'm sorry. I'm a selfish cow. I love you and I hope your day gets better xxx

I wait for a few minutes, hoping he'll respond. Finally, my phone beeps.

It's OK. I'm sorry. Love you xxx

Breathing a sigh of relief, I take the shopping into the kitchen. As I turn on the oven and tear open the oven chips, I know I should have bought that chicken. Never mind. We made up. That's one problem dealt with and now I just need to turn my attention to the other one.

May 21st

A few days have passed since Ailene called me and said she was declining my offer to have her to stay. She took the decision out of my hands and I'm grateful for that. We agreed we'd get together soon. The conversation was amicable. No doubt, she had had some reservations about coming too.

It is nearly seven o'clock in the evening. I'm expecting Charlie home from work soon. Outside the night is thick with blackness. I sit at my office chair, looking out the widow. I've been here for some time, trying to muster the creativity to write something. Anything. But it's been useless. I wish I could lose myself in my work like I used to, but since the murders everything has changed.

I've changed.

Something in me died when my parents were killed. The irony is that I never realised they really meant anything to me. I was so busy feeling bitter. And that bitterness was channelled into creating dark works of fiction. Without that bitterness, I am unable to write.

The small income I made from writing will not be missed. When my vast inheritance comes through, we won't require it anymore. I suggested to Charlie that he retire and we start a business together. He likes the idea but refuses to quit until we have a solid plan. He said he'd go mad if he wasn't kept busy. I know that's true but I also suspect he likes financially contributing. It's a man thing, I suppose.

Today, I spent a lot of time preparing a feast for our supper. It's Tuesday night and he could do with being spoilt. Work has been stressing him, as have I.

I've got him his favourite bottle of wine and cooked an array of Indian dishes. The table has been laid with candles and little pots of pickle, to go with the poppadums. I've even made samosas from scratch. It's nice to be busy. It keeps me from worrying.

That strange policeman, Woolfson, called today. We speak about once a week. He keeps me up to date with any developments, of which there have been none. It's such an odd case. There is no apparent motive and no indication as to whom the perpetrator might be. It's as though someone woke up one morning and decided they needed to break into a random couple's house and murder them. It has crossed my mind that it could be a serial killer. It all sounds very Hollywood, but it's the only conclusion I can make. Will another sorry couple fall victim to this madman? I hope not, but it seems a possibility.

I shake my head, determined to stop thinking about it and decide to go back into the kitchen and continue preparing for dinner.

Just as I get up out of my office chair, I hear the door opening. I dash towards the sound, longing to give my darling a hug. As though he knew I needed cheering up, he's holding a bunch of yellow lilies in his hand. Silently, he hands them to me, a small smile at the corners of his mouth.

'They are lovely.' I kiss his lips and linger for a moment.

'Something smells good.' He peers towards the kitchen.

'I cooked your favourite.' Taking his hand, I lead him through the house towards the smell of spices cooking.

Charlie slips his work satchel off his shoulder and sits down at one of the kitchen chairs. I notice the dark bags under his eyes and realise how tired he is.

After turning down the heat of the oven, I move behind him and start to rub his shoulders. He gives a low pleasurable growl and leans his head forward onto his chest. My thumbs work the skin around his neck and I press hard into the tight muscles.

'You can keep this up *for weeks,* if you like,' he says, reaching his arms around behind him and grabbing my thighs. Planting a kiss on his neck, I notice the increasing number of grey flecks in his dark hair.

'Food first. That later.'

'Have I got time for a quick shower?' he asks.

'Yep. Go for it. I'll have a beer waiting for you when you get out.'

'Perfect.' Charlie gets up and leaves the kitchen, his bag still slumped on the floor where he dropped it. I pick it up and hang it on a hook in the hallway. He's always been hopeless at tidying up after himself. Not that I am much better.

Returning to the kitchen, I look through the glass oven door at the tandoori chicken roasting away. The colour looks good and I guess it should be ready in twenty minutes. That leaves me just enough time to make some chapatti and warm the rice and bhindi bhaji I prepared earlier. On the hob, a pot of yellow lentils bubble energetically while onions, garlic and spices sizzle in a frying pan next to it. The room fills with warm scented steam. I may not be any good at cleaning but at least I can cook. One thing ticked off the perfect housewife list.

From a cupboard in the far corner, the boiler kicks into action.

When Charlie reappears, I am elbow deep in flour. He sits down to drink a beer and munches on a poppadum.

'How was work?'

'Don't ask. I'm this close to punching the prick on the nose.'

I have learnt it is best not to get into that conversation.

'This weekend, shall we do something? Go somewhere?'

'Where do you want to go?'

'Oh I don't know. Maybe take a boat down the Thames -anything.'

'Sure.' He brushes crumbs of poppadum from his mouth and the bib of his grey woollen jumper.

'Unless there's something you'd rather do.' I have kneaded and kneaded and the dough is nearly ready.

'You choose. I don't mind.'

His mind is elsewhere and a rush of irritation passes through me. I didn't go to all this effort for nothing.

'Might be a bit cold for a river cruise.'

'So, you do have a better idea?'

I'm finding it hard to hide my frustration. Then he says,

'We could get out of London. Maybe go to Brighton for the weekend.'

'That's not a bad idea. I could see if Soph's around to meet us for dinner.'

'Spoken to her recently?'

'Usual lots of emails back and forth. She's pretty wrapped up with this new fella. He sounds nice. We might get to meet him.'

'He can't be any worse than the last one.'

'That's for certain.' I mix the cooked lentils and spices, rapidly stirring with a wooden spoon before I get the chicken out of the oven. Three minutes rest and then dinner is served.

'I'm starving.' Charlie claps his hands together.

'I'll give Soph a call in the morning and see if she's free this weekend.'

'Cool. I'll book us into a decent B&B. We'll jump on a train on Friday when I've finished work.'

'Perfect.'

After dinner, with our bellies full, I roll a joint that we smoke outside on the bench in our patio garden. The night is cold and we watch our breath steam in front of our faces before disappearing into the black night.

For the first time in a while, I feel properly relaxed. I sit back and close my eyes for a moment. My hands are cold so I pull the sleeves of my green jumper down over my fingers and play with the soft fabric. My feet are cold too, so I cross my legs and curl my toes up under my bum. The hash is kicking in and the world starts to feel like a softer place.

When I open my eyes, I see Charlie is sitting forward, resting his arms on his knees and looking at the ground. I put my hand on his shoulder and lean in.

'Are you OK?'

He sits back, forcing me to retract my hand.

'Let's go in.' Charlie stands up. I nod and follow him back into the kitchen.

'Fancy another glass of red?'.

'Go on then. Bring it through. Let's sit on the sofa.'

I grab a pack of chocolate biscuits and tuck them under my arm and grasp the two glasses in my hands.

Charlie is already sitting on our old sofa, a frown plastered across his face. I hand him his wine and sink back into the cushions before taking a long sip of my own. There is a long silence, then,

'Jo, we need to talk.'

'OK.'

Butterflies start to flap in my stomach. I don't like his tone.

'Your parents…' I immediately feel myself tense. He turns to look at me. 'We need to talk about what's happened.'

'Charlie please, there's nothing to say now. The police are dealing with It.. I just want to try and have a normal life.'

'I'm not talking about that.' He speaks in a half whisper.

'What are you talking about then?'

'Your father.' His brown eyes slowly meet mine.

'What about him?' My voice has a quiver in it.

'You need to talk about it. About what he did.'

I bring my knees up under my chin and hug my skinny legs. Resting my forehead on my knees, a wave of ginger hair falls down and obscures my face. I close my eyes.

'Do you really want to do this right now? We were having such a nice evening.'

He picks up his glass and looks into the bowl. I look up. The red wine is sloshing from side to side, catching the light and reminding me of blood.

'You can't ignore this. It will catch up with you one day.'

'It caught up with me back then. I'm just beginning to move on. Why the fuck do you want to drag this all up now?'

'Josie, I love you. I know you don't like to talk about it but with everything that has happened, I really think you should. Just open up to me, let me know what's going on in that head of yours.'

He strokes my cheek with the back of his large soft hand. I don't mean to but I flinch. The hurt in his face is unmistakeable. I should feel sorry, but a rage is building inside me.

'OK, let's.' I slam my glass down on the coffee table, spilling some wine on the wooden tabletop and the cuff of my jumper. 'Shit.' I rub furiously at the stain.

'I'm not trying to stir anything up.' He is on the defensive, 'but I really think it's unhealthy to ignore this.'

'Right.' Now I'm on my feet with my arms crossed tightly across my chest. 'Let's talk about it then. Where would you like to begin?'

'Don't be like this.'

He rolls his eyes and sits back on the sofa.

'No, come on then, where would you like me to start? Perhaps I could tell you all about the first time the bastard crept into my bedroom and slid his hand under the covers. Or would you like to skip to the really juicy stuff? The first time he raped me, perhaps? Or the time he buggered me and I couldn't walk properly for a week.'

'Jo,' Charlie leans forward and puts his head in his hands. 'Please, don't be like this.'

'Like what? You want to talk about it, so let's talk about it!' I'm shaking now and sickness heaves in my stomach. 'I told Mum and everyone at school that I'd hurt myself falling off my pony. The pony *he* got me in order to keep me quiet.'

'Josie ...' Charlie gets to his feet and moves towards me with his arms open.

'No, don't. Why do you want to do this now? How is any of it going to help? You know all this fucking stuff.

All the sordid details - Why make me relive them?' I can feel tears in the corner of my eyes.

'I just want you to let it out. I'm trying to help.' He sits back on the sofa, defeated.

'Reliving the years of abuse I suffered at the hands of that animal, isn't going to do me any good. He's dead now. At last, the fucker is out of my life for good. Finally, I can start to lie the past to rest. Let's just leave it there, where it belongs. In the bloody past.'

'OK OK.' Charlie picks up his glass and drains the remains. 'I'm sorry,' he says finally.

I wipe a tear from my cheek and turn to face the wood burner. The fire isn't on, but I wish it were so that I could lose myself in the flames.

'I'm going up to bed. Are you coming?' Charlie moves towards the door.

'No, I'm not.' I can't look at him. 'I think I'll sleep on the sofa tonight.'

Although I do not turn to look, I sense him hovering by the door.

'Please, come on.' He sounds so tired.

'No. I'm too angry. It's fine. I'll get over it but just leave me alone now. I want to be by myself tonight.'

I hear him sigh.

'I love you, Jo.'

'I love you, too.' I can feel the tears returning. 'Sweet dreams.'

May 24th

By the time Friday comes around, things between Charlie and I have improved. I apologised for being a prickly bitch, and he said he was sorry for pushing the subject. I hope that from now on, he will leave the past alone and let me start to heal.

As I stand in our bedroom, deciding what to pack for the weekend, I feel an unfamiliar excitement. I haven't seen Sophie for some time and am looking forward to spending the weekend in her company.

She is my oldest friend. We were at boarding school together as teenagers and formed a firm friendship. In some ways, we are polar opposites, in others, like twins.

Sophie is much more academic than me and did very well in her exams. After Sixth Form, our paths went in different directions. She went to Oxford to read law and I ended up in Nottingham studying English Literature. She left university with a first. I came out with a very average 2:2. Now, she is a top prosecuting lawyer who lives in Brighton and commutes to work in London.

In practically every way, Sophie's a success. Her failures have only ever been her choice in men. She has jumped from relationships with abusers to losers, and back again. I really want her new flame to show more promise.

Standing in the spring sunlight flooding through the bedroom window, I gaze at the mass of crumpled clothes lying on the chair. Particles of dust dance in the haze, while I search for my favourite jeans. I've already packed my toothbrush and pants, now all I need are some clothes.

Sophie is always immaculately turned out.. Her clothes are perfectly ironed and she is the pinnacle of chic. I can't help but look as if I'd been dragged backwards through a bush, no matter how hard I try. But I have grown to be comfortable with my own chaotic, hippy style. This is who I am.

Finally, I decide to throw in an old, beige cashmere jumper, my pj's for slopping around in, a black cotton maxi dress and a duck egg blue, chunky knit cardigan. I pack my brown leather boots and slip into my Converse trainers, lying kicked off under the bed. Glancing at myself in my dressing table mirror, I rub a little blusher onto my cheeks and run a brush through my shoulder length ginger hair. For a moment, I see Ailene's reflection staring back at me. Then, the image disappears and I am left looking at myself. I hope she isn't frightened.

I check my wristwatch. It is nearly three o'clock. I am meant to meet Charlie at Victoria Station at half past six. If I leave at five thirty, I will have plenty of time to make the tube journey. I hate travelling in rush hour but it can't be helped.

I grab my bag and close the creaking, bedroom door behind me before making my way down the narrow staircase. In the kitchen, I empty the contents of the sink into the dishwasher and perform a cursory wipe down of all the surfaces. I flick the kettle on, make myself a coffee and slip outside for a cigarette.

The warmth in the spring air surprises me. I listen to the sound of sirens whirling in the distance, just another day in the big city. Rubbing my legs together, I puff hard on the cigarette and inspect the various pots scattered around the patio. They are pathetic looking. I am no gardener no matter how hard I try. Everything I plant and attempt to grow dies a sad, shrivelled death. Taking my last drag of the cigarette, I flick the butt into a far corner and go back indoors.

I still have a few hours to kill before it is time to leave, so decide to go and try to write something at my desk. There is an idea that has been brewing in the back of my mind for some time. Perhaps now is a good time to try and put something concrete down.

Sinking into my office chair, a cold shiver runs down my spine as the skin on my neck makes contact with the cold leather. Writing anything now is hopeless. I am struck by a sudden desire to sleep. Gingerly, I lift myself out of the chair and take tentative steps towards the sofa in the living room. Removing my mobile phone from my pocket, I set an alarm for five o'clock before resting my head on a dusty smelling cushion, pulling a blanket up under my chin and closing my heavy eyes.

The train takes an hour to travel in the darkness from Victoria to Brighton. Charlie and I share a bottle of Prosecco and some nibbles on route. He's always hungry when he finishes work.

We have arranged to meet Soph and her new flame at a restaurant at eight thirty. Hopping off the train, we make our way through the station before stepping out into the cold and hailing a cab. It takes five minutes to get to "The Set", on Regency Square. Charlie pays the driver and we get out of the silver Vauxhall, lugging our weekend bags

The restaurant is within a quirky, boutique hotel called the Artists' Residence. The hotel prides itself on having twelve rooms, individually designed by artists. The exterior of the building is typical to Brighton, with cream, painted stone walls, black metal railings and small balconies. The front door is painted shocking pink and makes me instantly cheerful. Sophie chose the place thinking of me. She knows I have a soft spot for bright, even garish, colours. She's so thoughtful.

We go into the reception where a friendly young girl with a nose piercing, offers to store our bags while we eat. She shows us through to the restaurant.

I'm very impressed. Entering through reclaimed doors, we are greeted by a small intimate room, with space for no more than twenty diners. The kitchen is open plan and I watch the chefs prepare dishes. The girl leaves and a tall, skinny, gay man, with short bleached hair, shows us to our table.

Sitting down in the fashionable, vintage wood and metal school chairs, I give Charlie a smile. It's so nice being out of London, away from the ghosts. The waiter saunters off leaving us to study the seasonal tasting menu. There are three tasting menu options, each offering four courses. Spotting rabbit as one of the dishes, my mind is made up. Without a doubt, I know Charlie will opt for the menu containing sirloin steak.

I feel relaxed and sit back in my chair to take in the rest of the room. Despite its size, the restaurant is buzzing. People are chattering loudly at their tables and bonhomie pervades the air, mingling with the sounds of cooking. The walls are a mix of exposed brickwork and wooden cladding. The lights hang low over the tables, their metal shades creating a warm light below.

I watch the entrance and on cue, my precious Soph appears accompanied by a stocky bearded man wearing a tweed jacket. Her face lights up when she sees me, and she dashes across the restaurant floor to greet me with a hug.

'So, so good to see you, Jo!' Her dark hair cascades down her shoulders and back, and I get a mouthful of it as we embrace. She smells of perfume and soap.

'Too fucking long.' I pull away and get a good look at her as Charlie stands and leans over the table to welcome her with a kiss on the cheek.

'Charlie, great to see you.' She beams. She looks so happy. I presume her companion may be the reason.

'This is Rory,' Sophie smiles at the bearded man and unwraps a soft, baby pink pashmina from her shoulders.

'Very nice to meet you, Rory.' Charlie extends a manly handshake.

'I'm Josie.' I say as enthusiastically as I can, willing myself to reserve judgement.

'I've heard a lot about you.' He sounds nice enough. No signs of being a wife-beater yet. 'Good to meet you at last.'

'I'm looking forward to getting to know you.' I sense a warning stare from Charlie who stands beside me. 'Now, let's all sit down and order some drinks. I'm parched.'

'When are you ever not parched?' Sophie twinkles.

'The last time was probably 1998.' We chuckle in unison. 'This place looks great. Been here before?'

'We came a few weeks ago. It's a little gem, isn't it? Started as a pop-up but has taken up permanent residence in the hotel due to its popularity. The food is to die for.'

'The menu looks great.'

'Right, who fancies Champagne?',

The white gold bracelets on Sophie's wrists jangle as she summons a waiter. Charlie flashes me a look to say, "I'm not looking forward to the bill at the end of the night."

'This evening is on me.' Sophie reads his mind and relieves the furrowed look from Charlie's brow.

'She's so generous, isn't she?' Rory chips in. I can't help it. I dislike him already.

'Champagne would be lovely. Thanks, Soph.' I ignore the creepy remark.

'Pleasure, Doll.' She winks at me. Her mascara and eyeliner are impeccably applied to accentuate the almond shape of her dark brown eyes. I am happy to accept her offer. She knows I will return the favour at some point.

'So, Rory, what do you do?' I examine his face properly for the first time. At a guess, I'd say he was in his early forties. He is handsome, in a way. His pale blue eyes stare out of his bearded face. He has a trilby hat on. I don't like the black and white dogtooth fabric it's made of. He's too old to be wearing something like that. Such things should be reserved for trendy teenagers or gay men. His thin lips curl into a small smile before answering.

'I'm a swimming teacher.' He fixes me with a gaze that makes me feel uncomfortable. I look away.

'That's surprising.' I raise an eyebrow. He fires back.

'Why?'

'Unusual, I mean.'

'Why?'

'I don't know, really.' I look to Charlie for help who doesn't pick up on it. 'I've never met a swimming teacher before.'

'We don't bite,' he smiles, picking up Sophie's hand and kissing the back of it lightly. She laughs. I don't.

'Have you always been a swimming teacher?' Charlie asks.

'That and nothing else.'

I can't understand why he seems so smug about it. He's a grown man who teaches kids how to swim. Hardly a rocket scientist.

'Oh.' Charlie is also dumbstruck. 'You must like your job.'

'I love it.' Rory's eyes light up. 'It's the best job in the world.' Something about the expression on his face leaves me feeling uneasy. 'It's so special being with kids in the water all day.' For a brief second, I am reminded of my father. I don't like what my brain is up to.

'So, tell me, how did you two meet?' I lean forward and change the subject, unable to look at him.

'Online.' Sophie says simply.

'A dating website?' I can't hide my surprise.

'Everyone's doing it nowadays. The site matches people for you and sends you your matches. Then you decide which one takes your fancy. And this one,' she says, pulling on Rory's sleeve, 'took mine.'

She nuzzles her face into his neck and I look away. It's so surprising to me that in this day and age, an attractive, young, successful woman needs turn to the Internet to find love.

Charlie, who has been looking at the menu for sometime, suddenly looks up.

'Shall we order?'

'I just don't like him.' I say. We are lying in our bed in our small hotel. 'I don't have to have a reason.'

'Yes love, I think you do.'

'Well, I don't have one.' Sitting up, I throw a pillow at him. 'I don't think he's trustworthy, OK? He seems too good to be true. And what kind of job is that for a grown man? There must be something wrong with him.'

'I thought he seemed decent enough.' Charlie pulls his jeans down and throws them over the back of a chair.

'You think everyone is decent, Charlie. I'm yet to meet a person you didn't like. Fuck, if Hitler came to dinner, you'd probably like him too.'

Charlie hurls the pillow back at me.

'I thought you loved that about me?' He feigns hurt.

'I do. You know I do.' I blow him a kiss.

'Just give the guy a chance, OK? Sophie seems happy. Maybe this one is a goodun.'

'Maybe.' But, I doubt it.

'You're so used to her boyfriends being shits, you've decided straightaway that this one is too, before even getting to know him. If you still feel that way by the end of the weekend, I'll concede. Deal?'

'Deal.' I smile. 'Now come and get into bed and service your wife.'

May 25th

The next morning, after a lazy walk along the pier and countless pounds wasted on slot machines, Charlie and I make our way towards Sophie's flat. She lives in the fashionable Kemp Town area of Brighton, very close to the beach.

I press the doorbell and we wait to be buzzed in. Sophie has the penthouse apartment in a lovely Victorian building, which is home to two other flats.

We slog our way up the many stairs it takes to get to her front door and knock. Rory opens the door, a smile plastered across his smug face.

'Welcome, folks. Looks like you made it just before the rain comes.'

'Hello again, Rory. Bloody awful weather for the time of year.' The men exchange a warm handshake.

As I step in, I'm hit by the delicious smell of lamb roasting.

'Josie, lovely to see you.' Rory gives me a hug.

'Likewise.' I answer, flashing a look at Charlie.

'Sophie's in the kitchen.' Rory takes a step back and gestures for us to go through. 'Can I take your coat?'

'No thanks, I'll wait till I've warmed up a bit.' I try not to sound curt as Charlie's words whirl around my head.

'Something smells good.' Charlie looks at me and raises his eyebrows.

'I hope you both like lamb.' Rory looks like a puppy waiting for praise.

We follow him into a vast, open-plan room.

'Doll! Right on time.' Sophie slides out from behind the workstation at the kitchen end. She is dressed impeccably as always. Her dark hair is piled on her head and large silver earrings dancing from her lobes. We share a hug before I slide onto one of the sleek black leather bar stools.

'Rory is cooking for us. He's a great cook.'

'Great.' Charlie gives Sophie a kiss on the cheek. 'I love lamb.'

'You love all food.' I say poking fun at my husband, who is handed a beer by Rory.

'What can I get you to drink?' Rory asks turning to me. He looks much better today without that stupid hat on.

'I'll have a beer, please.' I start to unwind my chunky knit orange scarf from my neck. Sophie stands, leaning against the white wall, sipping a large glass of chardonnay.

'I've got some nibbles in the fridge. Anyone peckish?' Sophie saunters towards the large chrome American style fridge, her hips swinging in her fitted grey denims. She is curvy, unlike me. I'm a ginger twig. She has breasts and hips. I've always envied her figure.

'Starving.' I sip on the bottle of beer.

'Tuck in.' Sophie produces humus, pitta, olives and nuts.

'Don't mind if I do.' Charlie gets up from the large, black, leather sofa and makes a beeline towards the snacks.

The room is an all-in-one kitchen, diner and living room. At one end is the modern kitchen, with white cupboards and chrome fittings. One work surface juts out slightly separating it from the rest of the room. Four expensive bar stools are lined up against it, perfect for entertaining.

The room is bright and has two huge windows that look out over the rooftops of Brighton. The floor has striped oak floorboards.

Near the kitchen area is a rectangular, elm wood dining table with a glass top that seats six. In its centre sits a large vase of white lilies, pride of place.

At the other end of the room are two black Le Corbusier sofas, with cream sheepskin cushions, a large flat screen television, and a solid oak coffee table. Against one of the clean white walls, a bookshelf contains law reference books and novels.

Her home, like her appearance is classic and chic. There is none of the clutter that sits about in my house. No sign of dust and no stains anywhere. Despite the length of time I've known her, I still find it slightly difficult to relax in her place. It's not that it isn't comfortable, it's just that I worry I might break something. Her taste is expensive.

Charlie is sitting back on the sofa now, glued to his mobile. I know exactly what he's up to. Checking the Liverpool score.

'Soph, would you mind terribly if Charlie turned the football on? It's just that it's a really big game. It'll be over by the time we eat.'

Charlie's head bobs up and he flashes a look at me that is a mixture of embarrassment and hope.

'Not at all. Rory, would you get the channel up for him?'

Rory is poking about in the oven with a meat thermometer.

'Be with you in a tick, mate.' Rory calls out, closing the oven door. 'Who's your team?'

'Liverpool. You a footie fan?' Charlie is anticipating the moment the television will be switched on.

'West ham, born and bred.' Rory throws the oven glove over his shoulder and marches towards the TV.

The men sit down, both holding beers and we watch as they lose themselves instantly in the game.

'They seem to have hit it off.' Sophie sits down on a stool next to me.

'Uh-huh.' I sip my beer. 'He's very at home here.' I feel her tense slightly.

'We've been seeing each other for a few months now. That's how it should be.'

I watch the men watching the television.

'Going well, is it?'

'Brilliantly. He's wonderful. I think at last I might have found my Charlie.'

'Wow. So it's serious, then?' I swallow hard.

'Very.' Sophie puts her wine glass down and turns to me.

'Soph, what's up?'

'You don't like him very much, do you?'

'Well, I ...' I trip over my words, '...I hardly know him.'

'You can't bullshit me, Jose.' She looks me in the eye.

'I'm not trying to.' I feel defensive.

'Look, I know better than anyone what bloody disasters my previous relationships have been. I know you all think I can't tell a diamond from a dog poo. But this time, it's different. I love him, I really do and I think this might be it.' She picks up her glass and drains the contents. 'We are living together.'

'Already? Here?' I can't hide my disapproval.

'Yes. He moved in a month ago. We've been discussing marriage.'

'Bloody hell! You don't hang about.' I'm speechless. She's never kept secrets from me before. 'I don't know what to say.' I turn to face her. 'Why didn't you tell me?' Suddenly, I feel hurt.

'Jose,' she says taking my hand, 'you have had so much to deal with over the last few months. So much pain. I guess I felt guilty for feeling happy. It didn't seem right that I was so happy when you have been so, so sad.'

'But you can tell me anything, you know that.' I'm talking to Sophie but looking at Rory and wondering just how quickly he managed to get his feet under her expensive table.

'I wanted you to meet him but you couldn't get to Brighton until now. Things just progressed and I wanted to tell you face to face. Besides, I knew you'd be protective and I thought if I told you on the phone you'd only worry. But now you've met him, you can see everything is just fine. He's lovely. Really he is. He would never hurt me.'

There is a long silence between us.

'You're like a sister to me. The sister I never had. If you say he's good enough then I accept it.'

In an unusual show of affection, she wraps her arms around my neck and gives me a huge squeeze.

'Oh Jose. You're a star. I accept that you can't trust him straight away but at least trust me.'

We smile and I see tears gather in the corners of her eyes.

'I trust you with my life, you silly cow. But look, if he steps even a millimetre out of line, I'll break his fucking balls. Got it?'

'Break his balls?' Sophie cackles. 'Got it. But he won't.' She seems so sure; her certainty is infectious.

'How are your folks? And your brother?' I ask.

'Very well. Pa is having a new knee in a couple of weeks. Other than that they are fine. Will is very well. He and Verity are expecting their second child in October.'

'They don't hang about, do they? How old is little Bella?'

'Nearly one.' Sophie puts her finger in her drink and pushes the ice cubes around.

Will, Sophie's older brother and only sibling lives miles away in Worcestershire. He's a farmer with acres of land and a nice, if not slightly dull, wife. They have bucket-loads of money and live a very comfortable life.

Sophie's parents, Annie and Marcus, also live in that part of the world. They are lovely people who were always very kind to me. I used to envy their family and wish I had one like it.

'Got anything else to drink?' I ask, finishing my beer.

'Plenty. What's your poison?' She hops off the stool, her boots echoing on the wooden floor as she moves into the kitchen.

'Got any of that Polish vodka you had last time I was here?'

'Absolutely. Double, is it?'

'You know me.'

'Have there been any developments with the case?'

The sudden change of conversation comes as shock to me. I don't want to talk about this now. I came to Brighton to forget.

'Nothing.' I say and stiffen in my seat.

'You know you won't be able to bury them until someone is arrested and there has been a court case? The police have to give the defence an opportunity to do their own examination of the bodies. It could be some time.' She's back to being a lawyer.

'Yes, I know.' I fold my arms across my chest and look out of the window. Sophie notes my reaction and backs off.

'Double, it is.'

June 3rd

We've been back in London for over a week. Our time away in Brighton did us the world of good. Seeing Sophie was like having an injection of fresh air, despite the tepid addition of Rory.

Now, I am sucked back into the real world. Yesterday, I received a call from the executor of the will. Since I am the sole beneficiary, everything has to come through me. Mr Potts, my parents' stuffy old lawyer, suggested that I thought about packing up and selling the estate. He said the sooner it was done, the quicker he could get the ball rolling. I had to agree to do it but hate having the responsibility on my shoulders. I just want to crawl under my duvet and die. The last thing I want to do is return to that house. There are too many bad memories and far too many ghosts.

I talked to Charlie about it two nights ago. He offered to come with me, to take more time off work, but I told him to stay. I'm sure it is going to take at least a week to work my way through every room. He can join me there at the weekend. There is no point in antagonising his arsehole boss any further. He had a good idea, which was to rope in Margaret to help me. She'd be grateful for the extra cash, no doubt, plus she has insider knowledge of the place and, also, that way, I wouldn't be alone. I love how Charlie's mind works. Sometimes he can be so practical.

I called her yesterday morning and put forward the offer. She jumped at the chance to earn some money. She's a nice lady, who 'did' for them for as long as I can remember but I suspect the idea of going through their personal belongings also appealed to her. The world the rich live in is somewhat of a mystery to most people.

I will definitely get her to go through my father's stuff. The idea of handling his clothes or anything that smells of him repulses me. At some point, I will have to choose the outfits they are to be buried in, but not yet.

So today, on this bright Monday morning, I am driving back to the house I grew up in. But, unlike most people, I don't enjoy the prospect of returning home. It fills me with dread and I felt this way long before it was the scene of a murder. I used to feel the walls were watching what my father did to me. As if, in some way, the house itself was complicit. Silly I know, but because of the size and age of the place, I was sure it was haunted when I was little and convinced the ghosts witnessed my abuse.

Now, I have to return to those ghosts again. Only now, there are two more who haunt the corridors. I shudder behind the wheel and turn the radio on, determined to drown out my ghoulish thoughts.

It takes three hours to drive from East London to the house, situated just outside of the small village of Bisley, tucked in the hills between Stroud and Gloucester. The region is well known for its Cotswold stone buildings and

the countryside is littered with chocolate box villages and crumbling stonewalls that separate the fields of grazing cows and sheep. The rolling hills are the backdrop to some magnificent views. It's no wonder so many of the rich favour this part of the England.

Once I had grown up and flown the nest, I had been able to see the beauty of it all. It is not a place that keeps you down, it is the people that live there. Returning to Gloucestershire at the end of every term, knowing I would have to spend the holiday holed up in that house, forever dreading the next time my father crept into my room, used to put the fear of God into me.

As I turn onto the long gravel driveway, I feel a strange sense of peace. The house that once kept me prisoner is now his prison. He can never leave.

The sun is shining through low, silver clouds that float lazy across the blue summer sky. I can't remember the sun ever shining here before. In my memory, it was always a grey place.

The manor has seven bedrooms, four bathrooms, five reception rooms and many outbuildings, including stables. At a guess, it's worth five million. I should be pleased knowing I've got all that money coming to me. But I'm not. I haven't taken a penny off them since leaving university, despite their offers. I don't want their money, now. Charlie said I am being too righteous. He thinks I should look at it as compensation. He's probably right.

I park the blue hatchback in the vast gravel driveway that sweeps in front of the house. I walk around the house towards the back door, the sound of my feet crunch as I walk, just as they always did. From my pocket, I remove my set of keys and open the door. The space is still boarded up where the glass once was. I am coming into the house the same way as the murderer. The thought makes my skin crawl.

The kitchen feels as vast and unwelcoming as ever it did when I was a child. More like a show room than a home. I cross it to sit down at the long pine table by the French windows and decide I'll wait for Margaret to show up. The house is strangely silent. As I look around the room, it dawns on me what a huge task lays ahead. The kitchen alone is full of things to go through. On the far side is a large French dresser. On its many shelves, an expensive gold and cream dinner service is displayed. I go over to it and pick up one of the plates. It feels cold and smooth in my hand. I turn it over and look at the emblem printed on the back. In green lettering are the words, Rosenthal, Germany, Aida. It doesn't mean anything to me, but I'm curious none the less.

Like most things in the house, it probably belonged to my grandmother. Fiona, my adoptive mother, inherited the place from her parents. Unlike Harold, my father, who was gauche and liked flashy things, she came from old money. No doubt, he was drawn to her because of it. I'm not sure he really loved her at all. I think their entire marriage was a show.

I put the plate back carefully and go over to the door to the vast walk-in larder. As I open the door and peer into the blackness, I hear a small knock behind me. Through the window, I can see Margaret standing, already in her apron, eagerly waiting to be let inside.

I open the door; she leaps forward and hugs me tight. She smells like mothballs.

'Oh, my girl.' Her voice trembles. She lets go and takes a step back to look at me.

'It's OK, Mags, really.' That is what I always called her when I lived there. It feels strange now, saying it as an adult. I haven't seen her for years, but I don't want to go through the pretence with her. Enough time has passed now and I don't need to spend every waking moment in bits. 'It's good to see you. I like what you've done to your hair.'

She blushes and the skin around her grey eyes wrinkles as she smiles.

'My, what a beautiful girl you've grown into.' Clearly, she doesn't accept that I am now an adult. But that's fine. Why should I mind?

'Right. We've got a lot of work ahead of us.' I know it's rude but I don't want to waste time having a catch up. We can chat as we work. 'I think the first thing we should do is to go through all the food. Throw out what's rotten. You can take the rest home with you? No point in letting anything go to waste.'

'That's very kind, lamb.' She folds her hands in front of her tightly. 'I was just wondering,' she clears her throat, 'when the funeral might be?' She shifts on the spot looking awkward. I feel for her. It's a perfectly reasonable question.

'The truth is, I don't know, Mags. They can't be buried until the police have made an arrest and charged someone. It's not looking very promising at the moment. They don't seem to have a suspect. It's as if the person responsible just vanished into thin air.'

'How awful.' She shakes her head. 'It's not right. They need to be laid to rest. You poor girl.'

Truthfully, I am grateful not to have to worry about planning a funeral at the moment. I've got enough on my plate and the idea of having to face all their friends and listen patiently, while people tell me how wonderful they were, fills me with dread.

'Hmm.' It the only answer I have.

'Well, let's get on with this then, shall we?' She sounds jolly in an attempt to lift my spirits. 'I'll make a start with the fridge.'

I had actually thought ahead and arranged for some packing cases to be delivered to the house and when we finally finish in the kitchen, we have separated stuff into boxes, some to be sent to the auction house, others destined for charity. I leave Margaret in the library putting the books into boxes, while I ascend the stairs.

I arrive at the long, wide corridor and wander along it, passing my parents' bedroom as I go. The door is closed and a piece of police tape is fastened across it. I have no desire to go inside and I hurry past. Large oil paintings hang on the walls. One features a hunting scene. I stop and look at it. I always hated it as a child. Men in red coats, on horses, stand over the body of a fox being ripped apart by hounds. The blood of the animal is the brightest thing in the picture. I can't imagine why anyone would want such a thing in his or her home. Looking at it, I realise there's very little I actually want from the house. None of it is in my taste.

I pass two of the bathrooms and three guest bedrooms before I reach my room. I know that it is going to look the same as it always did but something stops me from going inside. I linger by the door and imagine my father doing the same thing. It makes me want to scream. Revolted by the idea, I finally push the door open and go in.

It is a large room with pale, pink wallpaper and two big windows that look out over the gardens. The thick, sumptuous pink curtain fabric hangs gathered by tiebacks and pools out onto the cream carpet. It's all so unlike me.

I go over to the bed and sit down on the edge. Sat up against the pillows, is my old teddy bear. I pull him towards me and wrap my arms around his fat belly. He will come home with me.

I used to cuddle that bear after my father left my room. He was my one solace. I will never forget the first special hug.

After that, I would put on layers and layers of clothes before getting into bed. Anything to slow down the inevitable.
When I first confided in Charlie, he asked me why I never spoke out. I told him I used to think it was normal. It was something that happened in every family but people didn't talk about it. No one ever told me it was wrong. Normal people don't take their young children aside and tell them that some adults like to abuse children. Then, as a young teenager I blamed myself. I was ashamed and felt as though I should know how to stop it. When I was fifteen, it did. He finally left me alone.

I approach my dressing table that sits against a wall opposite the bed. Sitting down on the antique stool, I open one of the drawers and begin fingering through my things. Postcards, old photographs, ticket stumps and other bits I deemed worth keeping all lie collected together. I remove a picture of Sophie and I looking young and gawky in our school uniforms. I remember that day and smile. We had been on a history trip to visit a castle. Folding the picture in half, I slip it into my pocket.

I remind myself that not every moment of my childhood was bad. There were some good moments, too. The best thing they ever did for me was to send me to that school. I got a good education and made some great friends. The realisation makes me stop and think.

Why did they send me to boarding school?

I have a memory of listening to an argument between my mother and father. I sat on the other side of his office door, listening to them go at it hammer and tongs.

He was livid that she had enrolled me for a boarding school. Even then, I understood the reason why. She was shouting at him, telling him what a wonderful opportunity it was for me to broaden my horizons. She even cursed once. I had never heard her swear before and I don't think I ever did again. She was angry with him for not agreeing to adopt another child. She said I was missing out on not having a sibling and that the best thing they could now do for me was to surround me by my peers.

Looking back, I am grateful to her for sticking to her guns. She was right, but I can't help thinking that she knew what my father was doing to me. She was so desperate to send me away. It is the only conclusion that I can draw. She loved me and she would have wanted me close, so it was a sacrifice for her on my behalf.

I will never know if she suspected or not. Part of me wants to think she did, so that I can be thankful she sent me away. The other side of me wants to hate her for not putting a stop to it and protecting me.

I used to wonder how he justified it to himself. He either persuaded himself it was OK or he didn't care. His actions altered me. I had the potential to have an amazing life. What was wrong with me? Why didn't I get a real mum and dad?

In the room that was the setting for so many awful times, I feel an intense sadness that I have not felt before. For the first time since she died, I realise I miss my mother.

June 28th

I can see the bitch through the window. She's just sittin' there, eatin' biscuits and watchin' the telly.

I'm standin' behind the trunk of a big, bare, chestnut tree, in the dark. Back in bloody Milton Keynes again. My hoodie's pulled up, to stop the worse of the soddin' breeze from hittin' my skull. The sound of the drops peltin' the concrete is like a hammer to my brain. When will this fuckin' English weather ever cease?

The gum I'm chewin' has lost its taste. It's just a hard rubber ball givin' my teeth somethin' to do. Anythin' to stop them chatterin'. I've been here for over an hour now. Watched her make her dinner, sit alone at the table and eat some shitty lookin' brown food. I bet I'd get a better meal in prison.

It's kind of strange to me that she'd sit there, in her flat, without the curtains closed, so exposed. Especially, after a break in. A little smile creeps across my face, as I imagine the anguish she must have felt after. Good. I want her to be on her toes. To know that there is someone out there pokin' about in her life. Maybe then she'll watch her step.

She looks pathetic sittin' there alone, the bluish light from the telly reflectin' against her pale face. I almost feel sorry for the poor old woman. Seems to me like she's thrown her life away. Spent it sewin' or cooped up in that dingy little flat, when she could have had a family, a life.

Tonight I'm not here to cause her harm. I'm just checkin' up. Makin' sure everythin' is as it should be.

I find myself at a bit of a loose end these days. What with the other folks out the way, I don't have much to do to fill my time. I check the papers and news regularly, makin' sure the fuckin' pigs aren't on to me. They are no nearer catchin' me now, than they were weeks ago. Dead end is how the press reports it. Again I smile, pleased with myself for gettin' away with it. It seems murder really ain't that complicated. A bit of forward plannin' and there you go. Piece of piss.

That gets me thinkin'. How many people are there in the world, able to pull the wool over the eyes of the law? I'm not thick, but I'm no genius either. If I can manage it, just imagine how many sick fucks there are wanderin' around. Can't be too careful nowadays. All sorts of freaks and weirdos out there.

A warm rush runs up from my toes to the top of my head, and almost instantly I feel a stirrin' in my groin. That's my cue to leave. Time to go home, I think as I take one last look at the shell of the woman sittin' gazin' at the telly. She'll be fine where she is ... for now.

July 21st

Charlie and I get back to being what we once were. Free and easy, no hang-ups. No real ones, anyway.

I've always been difficult, temperamental, and he's always been him. Funny, bright and sanctimonious. Always thinking he's right. He'll argue with a brick wall and tell you it's made of straw, if you give him a chance.

No one else I know shares his ability to drive me mad. Sometimes, I think I hate him. Maybe I do. But behind the anger and frustration, lies a lost man. And that is where we find our common ground.

Back in our little London bubble, we reconnect. Sex, food and music become part of our daily routine again. At last, I'm not a victim anymore. I'm a survivor. He is no longer my carer. He's my equal.

We pack away the horror of the murders, the police and the press conference. They disintegrate like cork in a bottle of rotten wine.

We smoke tons of pot again. I spend too much time in my pyjamas and like a loyal dog he still goes to work, day in day out. It's similar to being a student again, except behind the façade are two people who should know better.

This cannot last. I know that.

He knows that.

And yet, I can't help but be mesmerised by the intoxication that has taken over and refuses to let go.

All I want to do is go to sleep.

Please let me sleep and if I must wake, let the answers flood in and be lost with the daylight.

August 3rd

When I peel the covers back from my face, I'm blinded by the blazing summer light. The curtains are closed and I don't know where I am. There is something familiar though. The duvet smells of stale body odour or sweat, and the room feels like it's sinking under a wave of tired dust. I finally realise I'm at home and London has never felt so lonely.

Peace at last.

Except it isn't. My head is full of concrete and it takes me some time before I am able to lift my eyelids and examine the watch on my wrist.

10:44 a.m.

Shit.

I must have smoked and drank more than I realized.

Shit. Shit, shit. Where did Brighton go?

And for a moment, I feel sorry for myself. Poor little rich girl, with the murdered parents, couldn't handle reality so decided to take a trip to Wonderland. But I don't believe in white rabbits or black holes, so where does that leave me?

Then, like a punch to the throat, I remember that things are good.

I'm in love with Charlie. He loves me. I'm lucky.

Shit.

He's always telling me to stop swearing. Too tired to argue with myself, I fall asleep remembering that I always promise to try.

The shrill ringing of the phone wakes me. Groping about on the duvet, I find the source of irritation. I answer without looking at the screen.

'Hello?' my voice sounds as if I've smoked one hundred cigarettes in a day.

'Mrs Brewers?' He speaks quietly and sounds grave.

'Detective Woolfson?' I sit bolt upright in bed.

'Yes.' He pauses for a moment and I can sense his lack of ease. 'Is it a bad moment?'

Can he tell I am hung-over? Can he hear it in my voice?

'No,' I give a cough to clear my throat. 'Not at all.'

'Good. That's good. I just want to check if it's alright to come and see you with Kelly Malling?'

'Has something happened?' My heart is in my throat.

'No, not as such but that is what we need to discuss. Are you free this afternoon?'

'Yes. I am. What time?' I dread having to see the family liaison officer yet again.

'At about 4.30 p.m.?'

He is so clipped. This is the man who has seen the bodies of my parents. Talking to him feels strange.

'That's fine.'

'We'll see you then.'

'Ok.'

He hangs up.

This is the last thing I need today. I don't have the energy to play hostess to the police in a couple of hours. But I couldn't say no. It wouldn't look good.

First things first, I need to eat. I need to sober up and I need to shower. I stink and the house is probably a mess.

By the time they arrive, I have cleaned myself and the house enough to persuade them that I'm not a complete case. The fact that I haven't persuaded myself is neither here not there.

This feels like the sort of situation that calls for tea and I consider making a pot, but it's August so I offer them juice instead.

The three of us sit around the kitchen table sipping the flat cloudy lemonade in silence. The quiet is deafening.

'So how can I help you?' I roll the glass between my hands, the condensation sooths me.

Woolfson looks at Malling and she turns to me.

'We are making slow progress with this case, Josie. That can't be easy for you to hear. I know you must want an end to all this.' She stops and looks to Woolfson again, who is nodding encouragement. 'We have a suggestion that might help things along.' Kelly fiddles with a strand of dirty blonde hair that's come loose from her ponytail. 'We think an appeal would really help.' Sitting back in the chair, I can feel her waiting for me to absorb the news. 'A television appeal to the public for information.'

I look up at Woolfson who is examining my reaction with his stern, blue eyes.

'Although this is something we can do without you, it really helps to have a member of the family there. We need people to come forward and tell us what they know. Having you there on camera would really bring it home for any potential witnesses and even the perpetrator.'

'You want me to go on television and ask people to come forward?' I really, really wish I had something stronger than lemonade right now.

'Yes. We are sure it would help.'

Oh Christ.

'What would I need to do?' my hands are beginning to shake and I know it's not just nerves.

'Well,' Woolfson leans forward resting his arms on the table and folds his hands. 'There would be a press conference. I would give a statement regarding the crime and then you would appeal to the public for information.'

'Would I have to answer questions?' The thought makes me feel ill.

'No, no, not if you don't want to.' Kelly puts her hand on my shoulder. I wish she wouldn't.

'Right.' I don't have a choice. 'Ok.' I'm going to regret this. 'If you think it will help.'

'We think it will.' Enthusiastic, Kelly nods.

'Ok then. When do you want me to do this?'

'In a couple of days.' Woolfson cuts in still fixing me with his gaze. 'The sooner the better. It doesn't take long to arrange the press. They love this sort of thing.' Kelly flashes him a look of disapproval, which he ignores. 'It's important,' he continues, 'that the public are sympathetic towards you. Do you understand?'

'Of course I understand. Don't patronise me, please.' I snap without thinking.

'What the D.I. means,' Kelly says trying to calm the situation, 'is that we need you talk about your parents. Let people know that you loved them. That sort of thing.'

'I hope you don't expect me to go all Jerry Springer for you. I'm a private person. I keep my feelings to myself. I'll do the conference because I want this person caught. I want justice for them.' I eyeball Woolfson back wondering why he's being so callous.

'Good. We will get him. It's just a matter of time.' He smiles and gets up from the table. 'We'll be in touch.'

September 8th

By the time I sober up, it is Thursday morning. Charlie left for work hours ago. A small note scribbled on a scrap of paper lies folded on his empty pillow.

Sleep it off. Will call at lunch. Xx

No, 'I love you.' Not that I deserve it, but it would be nice.

Still feeling as if my head is in a clamp, I wrestle with myself to gain some control. If I delve enough, I'm sure to find some solace. Some place where I can re-write the wrongs that hang around my neck like a chain.

Burying my face in the pillow, I know I should get up. I haven't showered in days and without needing to go downstairs, I know the house is a dreadful mess.

I keep playing the press conference over and over in my head. I hated being in the spotlight. All those cameras and microphones pointed at me. People giving me pitying looks, like I was the victim. I wish this would end.

Woolfson kept to his word and did most of the talking.

Charlie was there holding my hand, encouraging me all the time. I don't know if I could have done it without him.

I told them I didn't want to answer any press questions. I would have found it too stressful. They said that was fine.

Real life isn't as easy as it used to be.

I need to stop feeling sorry for myself. It's time to get a grip. I must get back to writing. I groan and stretch out, my bare feet stick out beneath the duvet, feel the cold air and retract like snails into their shell. Just five more minutes in bed won't hurt.

October 15th

Just as I start to doze off again, the familiar buzz of my phone vibrating on the bedside table stirs me. Feeling about for it, my hand finds my mobile and brings it close to my face. I open one bloodshot eye to inspect the screen. Ailene's name glows. I sit up quickly, forgetting my delicate state and immediately regretting my haste. I stare at the name for a moment before deciding not to answer. I need a coffee or eight before facing my mother. I tell myself I'll call her after breakfast as I put the phone back down on the table and sit up in bed.

It's then that I realise I am still dressed, wearing my black leggings and green cashmere jumper that has a hole near the cuff of the sleeve. Shame washes over me again and I let my head drop, my mess of ginger hair meeting like curtains closing on a stage. Rubbing my face with the palm of my cold white hands, I resolve to put an end to the self-pity and get out of bed.

Throwing off the duvet, I slide my legs round and let my feet find the floor. The floorboards are smooth and cold and I scour the room for my socks, spotting them lying discarded near the chair of my dressing table. Darting across the cold floor, I grab and pull them on. A half empty glass of water on top of our chest of drawers tells me to drink it all in one go. It might soften the thumping in my head.

As I leave the bedroom, I grab an old, navy, towelling dressing gown off a hook on the back of the door and wrap it around myself. A bit warmer, I am ready to face going downstairs.

The house is strangely cold and I head straight to the thermostat on the wall in the hallway. I know it was Charlie who turned it off. He doesn't feel the cold like I do and he's always worrying about the cost of our bills.

I go into the living room and grimace. There are empty bottles and glasses left on the coffee table and other surfaces, accompanied by take away boxes and dirty plates. The house looks likes it's lived in by teenagers.

Thankfully, Charlie isn't a neat freak. If he was he would never have married me, but I wish that he had at least put some of the rubbish in the bin when he'd come downstairs this morning. He gets up for work hours before he needs to leave. In that time, all he has to do is eat his breakfast, have a shower and get dressed. I wonder what on earth he does every morning.

Before allowing myself coffee, I collect the dirty crockery and pile it into the sink. I empty the full, stinking ashtray into the bin, coughing as a cloud of ash erupts from it. I take a black bag and fill it with rubbish littered in the kitchen and the living room. It only takes me ten minutes to make the house appear presentable again.

I am no longer feeling cold, so open a window. The stench of stale pot and tobacco hang in the air and cling to the rugs and upholstery. I duck into the kitchen and reward myself with a large mug of steaming black coffee. Its effect helps me begin to feel human again.

Sitting down at the kitchen table, I brush away some crumbs with the palm of my hand and wrap my fingers around the ceramic grey mug for warmth. I look out of the window. Outside, the sun is shining on the remaining yellow leaves of the pot plants I didn't manage to kill over the summer. I feel calmer now and ready to call Ailene.

I take my phone out of the dressing gown pocket and go to missed calls. Staring at her name for a while, I wonder whether I should change the contact to Mum, but, as I press the button and make the call, decide it's too soon.

'Hello?' Her faint Irish twang travels down the line.

'Hi, Ailene. I missed your call earlier,' I still get nervous when talking to her.

'Ah, yes. Josie, how are you?'

'Well, thanks. Charlie and I had a lovely weekend recently. It's good to get away sometimes. How are you? Any news on the break in?' I know it's been months, but I also know that it still plays on her mind.

'No, not a word from the Police. They seem certain it was hooligans, probably looking for something to do.'

'And how are you feeling? When we last spoke you mentioned you were still feeling uneasy.'

'I was, but I'm much calmer now. I've got my home back. A friend from the sewing shop came over and helped me reorganise. The furniture has been moved round. It makes it feel like a different place. I feel much better, now.'

I'm relieved that she seems to have got over it. Guilt lingered with me for a while afterwards for some reason. Perhaps, because I should have insisted she stayed with us. But now I can put that to bed.

'That's great.' There is a pause in the conversation while we both search for something appropriate to say.

'Getting ready for Christmas, are you?' she asks.

'I really hadn't thought about it. Is it that time already?' I rub my head wondering where the last few months have gone.

'Only a few weeks away, now. I like to go to church and help the priest hand out soup to the homeless at this time of year. People are so caught up in the commercial side of it that the true meaning of Christmas has been lost.'

'Hmm.' I can't get excited about church but her charity is to be admired. 'Very Christian of you.' I can feel the sarcasm creep into my voice that was there when I spoke to Rory. Charlie describes me as an atheist extremist. I think perhaps he's right. I try not to be so judgemental and soften my tone. 'What do you usually do at Christmas?'

'In the past, I've been back to Ireland, to visit distant family and the like but in recent years I've spent it at home.' The thought of her alone in Milton Keynes makes me feel very sad - a microwave meal for one and no presents to unwrap.

'Come here, this year.' The suggestion has left my mouth before my brain has had a chance to process it. 'It'll be fun.' I hear her give a little cough on the other end of the line and she says nothing. 'No one should be alone at Christmas.' I don't know if I'm succeeding, but I'm trying to reach out.

'Well, that's a very generous offer, Josie.' It still feels strange whenever she says my name. 'Why don't you have a word with Charlie and let me know what you decide. He might want you to spend it with his family.'

'His father is dead, his mother is ancient and in an old folks' home and his sister moved to Canada. I'm his only family. Please think about it.'

'That's ever so kind of you. I will. Thank you.'

'Well,' I say, stretching in my chair, 'I've got a lot to get on with today. I'd better stop chatting.' I dread saying goodbye. It is always uncomfortable. 'Let's speak again later in the week. Let me know what you decide.'

'Ok, I will.'

She sounds more like a head mistress again and I can hear that her barriers have gone up.

'Right, well, bye then.'

'Goodbye.' There is a click at the other end of the line and she has gone. I am left wondering if she found it that easy to walk away when I was born.

Shaking myself free from the thought, I decide it's time to wash away the grime from the last few days' gluttony and head upstairs to have a shower.

Shrugging the dressing gown off, I go back into my bedroom to replace it on the back of the door. Clothes strewn everywhere, drawers open, make-up lying all over my dressing table, empty glasses of water, a pile of discarded newspapers on the floor on Charlie's side, dust covering everything and an over-flowing laundry basket.

'Fuck it.' I say aloud. Before I shower, I know I need to tidy up. The first thing I need to do is change the bedding. The room has a faint smell of sex. We've been sleeping in those sheets for weeks.

I rip off the crumpled sheet, pillowcases and duvet cover, go onto the landing and throw them down the stairs to be washed later. From a cupboard by the bathroom, I pull out some fresh bedding; a clean, white cotton duvet set that was given as a wedding present.

Carefully unfolding the large sheet, I stretch it out and go around the mattress folding it tightly under every corner. As I pull it taut, my hand brushes against something fabric under our bed. Getting down on all fours, I tip my head to the side and peer beneath the bed.

In the darkness, I can just see the outline of a bag, the strap of which is sticking out from under the bed frame. It's well wedged at the back. If I hadn't felt the strap, I would never have known it was there. I give it a tug and slide it out into the light.

There is nothing remarkable about it but I don't recognise it. It's a plain black fabric rucksack. It must belong to Charlie I think, but I have no recognition of seeing him with it. I inspect it again, holding it up and looking at it from various angels. It's had some use, that's for sure. From the weight of it, there are things inside. Sitting on the ground, still in the clothes I wore yesterday, I fold my legs and unzip the bag. A strange feeling of dread grips my throat and I hold my breath as I remove the first item.

It's a porn mag, a well-used one at that. The cover is battered and the pages have been turned repeatedly. It must belong to Charlie. No wonder he hid it. This is his private stash.

I pop the dirty mag back into the bag feeling a mixture of relief and motherly disapproval. As my hand goes back into the rucksack, it is met with the touch of cold metal. An uncertain feeling floods over me as my fingers lock around the object. My heart is beating hard as I remove the heavy item from the bag. Taking it out, I lay it on the ground, not wanting to hold it and stare at a crowbar.

Why the fuck has Charlie got a crowbar under our bed?

The pornography I can understand but this makes no sense. Dumbstruck, I look at the cumbersome object trying to work it out. A threatening piece of equipment, its purpose is unclear.

Charlie has never been one for DIY, so I can rule that out. The question that echoes around my brain is '*why is it hidden?*'

I'd know if he were a burglar or thug. He isn't. He's my big, soft bear. But why does he have a crowbar hidden in a bag with a dirty mag? For a second, I wonder if it might belong to someone else. But *who*?

Confused and slightly scared by the discovery, I bundle the weapon into the rucksack and push it back far under the bed. There must be a rational explanation I tell myself, getting up and dusting off my knees. I trust Charlie. It's that simple. So, he has a porn mag. So what? But, it's not the magazine that's bothering me.

I leave our bedroom and go into the bathroom, pull back the curtain and turn on the shower. The room fills with hot steam in seconds. A long shower will make things better. Dropping my jumper and leggings onto the floor, I stand in my underwear for a minute waiting for the water temperature to be just right. Despite the heat clouding up in the room, I feel cold and all the tiny hairs on my body stand alert.

Slipping my nude coloured bra off my small pale breasts, I throw it onto the back of the loo, followed by the white knickers.

Stepping into the cascade of hot water, I let it soak my head. It snakes down my face mimicking tears and gathers in the corners of my mouth before tumbling down my chin. I close my eyes and listen to the sound of the torrent. It hammers the ceramic bath ferociously echoing the pounding that has returned to my head.

'Everything is fine.' I often speak to myself when I'm taking a shower, where no one can hear me. Sometimes, when you ask yourself questions, you find some surprising answers.

Reaching for the shampoo, I try to ignore the uncomfortable feeling swirling around in my stomach.

October 16th

'Of course you should invite her for Christmas. It's about time we met.' Charlie sips his glass of Shiraz and sits back to stare at the small flames licking in the wood burner.

'When shall we go and visit your mother?' I ask trying to conceal my dread.

'Don't know if there's much point anymore.' He cannot hide his sadness.

Betty, now ninety years old, lives in a care home not far from Coventry. She has been there for the last seven years. I never knew her before the dementia and Parkinson's Disease set in. To me, she has always been a frail, confused, old woman. But Charlie remembers her as she was, before old age got its claws into her. He tells stories of her when he was growing up. She worked in a cake shop part time and used to bring home sticky buns for tea. His father, Alan, had been in the navy but once retired spent most of his time either in the pub or at his allotment. I got the impression he wasn't a nice man. He died before Charlie and I met.

Betty, by Charlie's account, was a hard working, loving mother. She had three children. Charlie had an older sister, the one who now lives in Canada and a younger brother, Phil, who died at the age of eighteen. Charlie never talks about what happened, just says that he was ill. It seems Betty never recovered from the loss of her youngest son.

After Charlie had flown the nest, Alan finally drank himself to death, leaving Betty alone.

Since his sister emigrated, Charlie was the only one left to take care of their mother. He told me he offered to have her to live with him in London, when the early signs of Parkinson's reared their head. But she was a proud woman who kindly refused the offer from her son. When things got too much, Charlie found the best NHS home he could to care for her.

In the early days, he told me he used to visit every fortnight. Then, as her illness progressed it was once a month. Now, he calls her once a week, every Sunday afternoon and visits every three months. He cannot stand to see her in the state she is in and justifies it with the knowledge that the poor old girl has no idea what year it is. She no longer recognises him as her son nor anyone she has ever known.

'I might nip up there on the 23rd and spend an hour. You don't have to come.' Charlie dreads the visits too.

'I'll come.'

'No, don't. What's the point? She doesn't know you. Jesus, she doesn't even know me.'

'Look, I know how difficult it is for you and I want to be there for support.' It feels good not being selfish.

'That's sweet of you, love, but I'll be fine. You stay. Go mad decorating the house. You know you prefer it when I'm not under your feet.'

'Well, that's true.' I'm not going to force myself on him. 'But if you change your mind, just let me know. I can go crazy with the tinsel when you're at work.'

'No doubt you will.' He grins putting his glass down on the coffee table. 'So how long are we going to have your mother staying with us?'

'I hadn't got that far. I don't want to push it. Maybe if I ask her to come on Christmas Eve and stay until the 27th. What do you think? I think three nights is more than enough. If I could suggest two I would, but she doesn't drive and the trains are crap around Christmas.'

'Sounds fine to me.' The fact that Charlie is so laid back is one of the things I love about him.

'Great. I'll give her a call tomorrow and sort it out.' I sink back into the sofa cushions, enjoying the warmth of the fire on my outstretched feet. Charlie goes into the kitchen.

I scratch at a small brown stain on the seat of the sofa.

'Maybe when my inheritance comes through, we should buy a new sofa.' I call to him.

'Why not? Let's go wild.' He is mocking me. He comes back holding a bottle of Shiraz and a box of chocolates.

'Screw you.' I laugh. 'I'm going to be a very rich woman. You better watch your step, old man.'

'Less of the old man, thank you.' He sits down close to me, puts the wine on the table and hands me the box of Ferrero Roché. 'You're enjoying your chocolates at the moment.' He squeezes my thigh and opens the bottle of red.

'Calling me fat?' I shove a chocolate into my mouth and crunch down loudly. 'I always up my choccy intake in the winter. You know that.'

'Fair enough.' Charlie pours two large glasses and hands one to me. 'So,' he says changing the subject, 'what do you want for Christmas?'

'Oh, fuck knows.' I say with a mouth still full of chocolate. 'What about you?'

'I don't know. Maybe a new bag for work.'

'Don't be so dull. There must be something more exciting you'd like? A holiday, perhaps?'

'We can't afford that at the moment.'

'We will be able to soon enough.' I can't help but look forward to the large sum of money due.

'I don't know, love. Use your imagination. You always come up with something.'

'It's true, I do.'

'And, what about you? Some underwear perhaps?' He nuzzles his face into my neck and ever so gently grips the skin with his teeth, almost spilling his glass of wine as he does so.

'If you won't let me get a new sofa, you'd better be careful not to spill wine all over this one.' I pull away, smiling.

'Spoilsport.'

'Finish your glass first, then I'll show you exactly what this spoilsport is really made of.'

November 28th

I fuckin' hate Christmas. People walkin' about lookin' all smug and happy. Spendin' all their hard-earned money on fuckin' presents for people they don't give a shit about. It's a joke. A great, big, commercial joke.

As I make my way up Oxford Street, I brush shoulders with hundreds of strangers. No one looks at me in the eye and I'm grateful for that. If they did, I might have to smash their skulls in. I keep my head down and just keep walkin'. I focus on my trainers takin' one step at a time on the damp, dark pavement. Above me, the festive lights flash and in the distance I hear a bunch of fuckers singin' carols. Singin' about God. What god? Ignorant sheep, the lot of them.

I have no real direction I'm goin' in, just fancied a walk. But I'm regrettin' it now. The hustle and bustle hurts my head and the jolliness makes me sick.

I pass a middle-aged woman, carryin' expensive lookin' shoppin' bags. She's wearin' a fur coat and smells of sickly sweet perfume. Lookin' up, I see her face has seen better days. The money she's spent on Botox ain't done her any favours. The skin around her eyes is pulled tight and thick fake eyelashes look like two black caterpillars restin' on her face. The red lipstick is smudged and she has some on her teeth. I'm glad she looks as stupid as she does. Rich bitch. Freak.

I turn left onto Regent Street and head south. It's only the middle of the afternoon but already night is fallin'. Taxis clutterin' up the roads beepin' their horns at every given opportunity. I hate the buzz of people and traffic and wonder why the fuck I came into this hellhole.

As I pass Hamley's toyshop my pace is made even slower by the congregation of brats and their parents, hoverin' outside, starin' at the stupid displays in the windows. Fuckin' Christmas. No one ever got me nothin' from Hamley's. I never got taken to London to see the bright lights. They don't know how lucky they are.

A little boy, probably about eight or nine years old, is whingin' to his mum to go into the shop and buy him the latest toy. The mother, a tired lookin' wench, is tryin' not to lose her temper with the lad. I slow to listen to the conversation, even stoppin' for a moment and pretendin' to look in the window myself.

'Every one else at school has one. Please Mum, please, please.'

'No, Tom. Christmas is just around the corner. If you're very lucky, Santa might put something under the tree.'

'But I want it now.' The kid wipes a trail of snot across his cheek with his sleeve. 'Dad would get it for me if he was here.'

'Well, he isn't, is he?' Out of the corner of my eye, I watch the mother's face tighten. 'He's with his new family.'

'You're a real bitch.' The kid says before kickin' her in the calf.

'Don't you speak to me like that.' Other people have now stopped and are watchin' the drama unfold. 'I'm not made of money.'

I approach them smilin' and bend down, so I'm on a level with the kid.

'You know, Father Christmas only comes to good little boys and girls.' I tell the child who looks at me blankly.

'I'm not stupid. I know he's not real. It's just Mum and Dad pretending. I want it now.' I cock my head to one side and eyeball the boy. 'What is it to do with you? You're a weird-looking man.' The boy is totally un-fazed by me.

'Tom, enough!' His mother barks.

I lean in and whisper into his ear very quietly, so nobody else can hear.

'Listen, you little shit, you'd better apologise to your mum, or I'll creep down your chimney and glue your foul little mouth shut while you sleep.' Standin' up, I pat the terrified child on the head before turnin' to his weary lookin' mother. 'He's got somethin' to say to you.' I put my arm around his shoulder and grip tightly.

'I'm sorry, Mum.' The little boy bursts into tears, and runs over to his mother, burying his snotty face in her coat.

'That's better.' I take a step back and smile at them both. 'Merry Christmas.'

I can feel the woman starin' at me in disbelief as I cross the road and disappear into the crowd.

December 23rd

I love Christmas, everything about it. Ever since I was a little girl, it's always been my favourite time of year. Not because I like getting presents but because I love the idea of people coming together, families sharing food, singing songs and playing games.

As a child, Christmas was always an extravagant affair. My mother spent God knows how much money on decorating the house. The fireplace was always the centrepiece, with a huge custom-made garland hanging pride of place. The wreath on the front door seemed huge to me, with lots of red satin ribbon, mistletoe, pinecones and holly all carefully weaved together. The mahogany dining table was laid fit for a king. Crystal glasses, cream pillar candles, polished cutlery and a smart gold plated dinner set adorned the table.

Despite the lavish nature of the Christmases they hosted, I never felt part of a proper family. Being adopted and an only child made me feel like an outsider. It was a very formal affair with my adoptive parents. They lived on ceremony. Everything was for appearance's sake.

Looking back, I think my mother must have known what he did to me. She must have sensed my terror of him. How could she not? I became withdrawn from the moment he started to abuse me. The first time he crept into my bedroom, I was only eight years old.

The strange thing is that apart from the horror of sexual abuse, he was actually quite kind to me. I suppose he had to be in order to keep me on side. I was frightened of him, but I never thought he'd hit or punish me. I was his princess. He inflicted a different kind of pain and as I sit here thinking about it, I would so much rather he had hit me. Anything would have been preferable to those bedroom visits.

Determined not to let my jolly mood be spoilt by ghosts from my past, I put the thought of my adopted father to the back of my mind and continue hanging the glittering papier maché snowflakes on pieces of thread in our sitting room window. I made them myself a few years ago and display them every Christmas.

The windowpanes are icy to touch and my hot breath steams up on the glass. Outside, the indigo night enfolds the vast cold city.

Tomorrow, Ailene will arrive. It will be my first Christmas with my birth mother and I cannot hide my excitement. I feel like a small child again. Soon, Charlie will return from work and the celebrations can begin. It's a tradition of ours that we share a bottle of Prosecco and smoke some weed to welcome the start of the holiday.

The fridge is filled with artisan cheese I bought from Broadway Market, a foodie market in the heart of Hackney that has amazing fresh produce and lovely street food. It's full of hipsters walking in the rain wearing their expensive Ray Ban Wayfarers and sipping herbal tea, but that's part of the fun. The cheeses cost a small fortune.

My stomach rumbles as I move over to the wood burner and prod the small fire, stirring the flames back to life. The room has a warm glow and I admire the large Christmas tree standing in the corner, its white fairy glittering with pride. This is how it should be, I think while I get the cheese from the fridge and display it on a wooden board, along with crackers, home made chutney and purple grapes.

Looking up at the clock on the wall, Charlie should be home soon. He went out for drinks with some work colleagues but promised he'd be back by eight thirty. It's quarter past.

I think about rolling myself a joint but decide to wait for my husband. A glass of wine will do for now.

Padding back into the sitting room, the floorboards creaking beneath my slippers, holding my newly-filled glass, I move over to the wood burner, pic up a cushion, drop it on the floor and sit down near the fire. In a more wholesome household, I would be drinking hot cocoa, but it is Christmas after all. I take a large glug of Rioja.

I flick through my music on my phone, looking for something jolly to blast out the wireless speakers that I bought Charlie as a present last Christmas. I can hardly believe a year has passed. So much has happened. So much has changed. A few months ago, I didn't think it would be possible to be sitting here now, feeling happy. But that's life, I suppose. You never know what's around the corner, and when it appears, and punches you in the face, in time you adapt in the only way you can to the situation.

I come across the Rolling Stones greatest hits and settle on listening to that. The band may have been around long before I was born but their music remains timeless. Everyone loves the Stones, even if Mick Jagger is the world's biggest prick.

As *Jumping Jack Flash* comes to an end, the click of the front door lock sounds and I spring up off the floor to greet Charlie. He comes into the sitting room, unwinding an orange scarf from his neck and shaking off his coat.

'Happy Christmas!' I hold my glass up in the air and smile showing all my teeth.

'Not quite yet, love.' He drops his bag on one of the armchairs.

With those four simple words, my good mood evaporates. I know it's not Christmas day but the holidays have began. Surely, he knows what I mean?

'Bad day at work?' I put my glass down and fold my arms across my chest.

'Not that bad. Bloody tube was packed tighter than a tin of sardines.'

'Oh well,' I can feel my irritation growing, 'you're home now. No more commuting for the next week.'

I follow him into the kitchen and watch him pour himself a large glass of water and drink it in one go before speaking again.

'Food looks good.' He nods his head in the direction of the cheese board.

'I wanted to treat you.' I say, regretting the effort I've made.

'I'm going to jump in the shower. Wash that bloody tube off me. We'll eat when I come down, OK?' He pecks me on the cheek before leaving the room.

Disappointment floods over me as I go back into the sitting room and resume my position on the cushion. I no longer feel like listening to music and jab at my phone before chucking it onto the sofa. I hug my legs and stare at the flames licking around the charred, black wood.

I know he's tired, but for Christ's sake, can't he show just a little bit of enthusiasm? This is the start of the holidays for him. No more work or having to take the tube to work. That is something to celebrate, even if he doesn't really care about Christmas.

Sitting huddled on the floor, I wonder when he lost his sparkle. When we first met, he was so enthusiastic about life, always positive and carefree. He's never been exactly reckless but he enjoyed life and looked forward to what may come. Now, recently, he seems old to me. The spontaneous man I met, who would whisk me out to the pub on a Tuesday night despite an early start the next day, the guy who told me to leave the rat race and follow my dreams, the guy who proposed only after six months. Where has he gone? Now, he spends his time worrying about work and money. He seems to have forgotten how to have fun. He's become so sensible. I fear he's on the verge of becoming boring. I appreciate that there is an age gap between us, but that doesn't explain it and besides, I am about to inherit a fortune, so money is the least of our problems. He never has to work again, if he wants.

I drain my glass in one go. Fuck it. If he isn't going to join in, I'll make my own fun. From my cotton pyjama trousers pocket, I remove a little tin containing weed, tobacco and rolling papers. I roll a large joint. I'll smoke it without him I decide, heading for the back door in the kitchen. But when I reach it, I have a change of heart. I'm fed up with the way we always do this. It's bitterly cold outside, I'm in my slippers and it's Christmas. I am not going outside to smoke. Why should I? I pick up the cheese board and carry it through into the sitting room, the unlit joint hanging from my lips. I put the food down on the coffee table and return to my place on the floor near the fire. I lean over to a nearby basket containing small logs and remove a pack of matches.

Dragging the brown phosphorus tip against the rough edge of the cardboard box makes a delicious sound and I watch with fascination as the wood sparkles into life, finally settling as a small blue flame.

I put the end of the joint into the fire and inhale deeply. The earthy herb tastes good and I close my eyes allowing the warm drug to sink down into my lungs. Better already, I think opening my eyes and deciding I will listen to music after all. Appropriately, *Play with Fire* starts to boom out of the speakers and I smile.

Charlie will relax after he's had a shower, I hope. I'll just sit here enjoying the music and watch as the smoke circles up into the air, gathering in a layer of fog above my head. All he needs is a full glass, a full belly and a lungful. Then he'll be fine.

Charlie reappears, wearing his jeans and a brown jumper. I notice the growing collection of grey hairs on the sides of his face for the first time. He is aging well, I think and for a man in his fifties, he is still handsome. He stands in the doorway of the sitting room and stares at me with irritation.

'Have you been smoking in here?' He asks sniffing the air. 'Yes I have. I've rolled you one.' I brandish the joint in his direction. He doesn't take it.

'I thought we agreed we'd smoke outside.'

'Well, I changed my mind.' I sound like an obnoxious teenager.

'I hate the smell in the house.' A look of thunder crosses his face.

'I know you do. But it's freezing outside and it's only for tonight.' My arms are folded again in self-defence.

'So, put a coat on.' He sits down on the sofa and takes a cracker from the cheese board. 'Where are the plates?'

'In the kitchen cupboard where they live.' I scowl.

'Oh, grow up.' He pops a grape into his mouth and bites down hard. 'What the hell is wrong with you this evening?'

That is the last straw.

'Are you fucking kidding me? You come home with a face like a slapped arse and I'm the one with the problem?'

'Not true.' A vein on the side of his neck is pulsing, the way it always does when he's angry or lying.

'I made a special effort this evening. You came back, didn't even say hello or ask how my day was. Now, you're having a pop at me about smoking one joint in the house. This is my house too and if I want to smoke inside, I fucking well will.' By now, I'm standing on my feet and my voice is louder than I intended.

'Fine. Do what you like.' He picks up a knife and cuts violently into the soft Brie before smearing it on a cracker.

'Why are you being like this? It's the start of the holidays, I thought you'd be happy?'

'I just don't see why you couldn't smoke it outside.'

'You know what, I could have, but I decided that just for once, I would enjoy it in front of the warm fire. Stupidly, I thought you might think it was a good idea.' The lie trips off my tongue with ease. 'And it's not exactly hurting anyone. We don't have any kids in the house, we both enjoy a smoke, so what's the harm?'

'Good thing we don't have kids, if this is how you are going to behave.'

'Stop talking to me as though you're my father. What's happened to you? You used to be so much fun.' The anger is fading only to be replaced with a feeling of despair.

'I just wish you'd get your head out of the clouds and come back to earth. You're smoking all the time at the moment, drinking too much. You seem to have changed into someone else.' The bags under his eyes emphasize the sadness in them. 'I know you've been through a lot. More than anyone should ever have to go through, but I thought you were making progress.'

'I am. I have.' I protest sinking onto the sofa next to him and taking hold of his hand. 'Look, I'm sorry I was a bitch. I just wanted us to have fun tonight. To enjoy ourselves, like we used to. Is that so much to ask?' All the fight has left me.

Charlie cups my face in his hands and kisses my forehead.

'OK, OK. But you don't want Ailene to smell it when she arrives. Smoke in here tonight. Go on, hand me that joint. But tomorrow, we go back outside again. Deal?'

'Deal.' I kiss him, enjoying the taste of ripe Brie on his breath. 'But you have to do me a favour.' He is eyeballing the cheese and deciding which to attack next. 'No talk of work. Let's enjoy the time we've got together. It is Christmas after all.' I gesture at the spruce laden with gold and red baubles.

'Fine. Suits me.' He begins cutting into a large chunk of Stilton.

'And no more fighting?' I snuggle against his upper arm, enjoying the scent of fresh laundry coming from his jumper.

'Promise.' He says through a mouthful of cheese. 'Fun, fun and nothing but fun.'

December 24th

When I wake and sit up in bed, I take a sip from the glass of water on my bedside table, only noticing the thin rim of dust floating on the surface too late. My mouth tastes like a dry slug and I have a desperate urge to brush my teeth.

Like most mornings, Charlie is nowhere to be seen. I will find him downstairs, his breakfast of boiled egg and toast already finished, probably reading the paper or on his laptop while the BBC news reverberates from the television.

I curl up into a foetal position bringing my knees to my chest. I don't want to get out of bed. We should all be hibernating, I think to myself. But then the prospect of Christmas stirs me from my slumber and I am out of bed faster than a jackrabbit, barely noticing the cold floorboards and landscape of mist gathered on the windowpanes.

Despite my growing excitement, there is a cloud hanging over my head. I have the faintest memory of a bad dream, a violent and stressful nightmare that played in my head last night. The visions from the dream are unclear, shrouded in a cerebral fog, but there is a lingering sense of dread that I can't shake. I don't feel very well rested as I pad down the stairs, wrapping my dressing gown tightly around my skinny body.

As predicted, Charlie is on the sitting room sofa with one eye on his emails and the other on the news headlines. I ruffle his hair as I pass and he blows me a kiss over his shoulder.

'There's black coffee on the table.'

I nod with silent appreciation, head into the kitchen and make a beeline for the cafetière. The coffee is still acceptably warm and I pour the remains into a mug I take out of the dishwasher. It's bitter and strong and feels like the answer to a prayer.

'What's the plan for today?' Charlie calls from the sitting room.

'I need to make the spare room up. A few final bits of shopping to do, other than that, everything is pretty much done.'

'I need to pop out and buy some last minute things. Otherwise I'm all yours.'

'Sounds good to me.' I am starting to feel human again. The coffee is working its magic. 'Fancy lunch somewhere cheap and cheerful?'

'Why not.' I hear his fingers tapping on his keyboard. 'Anywhere in particular?'

'Erm,' I put my hands on my hips and frown at the floor. 'Let's try The Marksman pub on Hackney Road. I read an article praising the food. Fancy giving it a try?'

'Done.'

'Great. I'd better book as its Christmas Eve. Shall we say one o'clock?'

'Fine. I better get a move on, I suppose. I need to go into Central.'

'Are you bloody nuts? It's Christmas Eve. It will be heaving.'

'Ugh! I know, but it has to be done.'

'I never understand why you always leave your shopping until the very last minute.'

'Not all of us start planning Christmas in August, Jose. Some of us like to keep it a bit more relaxed.'

I huff and turn to the sink full of dirty plates and glasses.

The Quiet Ones

I pull up my sleeves and plunge my hands into the cold, dirty water, fumbling for the plug.

Humming a tune from an advert that has locked in my head, I unload the dishwasher and restack it. It's a tedious job, but it's mine none the less. As I bend down to put a glass in it, I almost jump out of my skin when Charlie wraps his arms around my waist.

'Fuck! Don't do that!'

'Sorry. Didn't mean to make you jump. Just letting you know I'm heading off. It makes sense to meet you at The Marksman. Saves me coming back here first.'

'Sure. No problem. One o'clock.'

'One o'clock,' he nods, grabbing his keys and wallet from a bowl on the kitchen table.

By the time I sit down at the pub table for lunch, I am a bag full of nerves. Today is the first time my husband and mother will meet and I really hope it goes well. There is no reason it won't, but I'm still a wreck.

I check my wristwatch. It's one fifteen and there is no sign of Charlie. Usually, he's good at being prompt, so I know to expect him soon.

The pub is busy. All the tables are full. In the corner of the room is a hearth where a fire blazes; occasional sparks jumping out of it onto the tiled surround. Christmas songs dance out of the small speakers on the wall and quietly I sing along, losing myself in the monotony of the words to distract my agitated mind. By the time Charlie arrives, I feel much calmer.

He smiles across the room and I wave back. In his hand, he is carrying a small plastic bag. Despite the hours he has spent shopping, it doesn't look very promising.

'Hi.' He bends down and kisses the top of my head. 'I'm gasping for a drink. Do you want another?'

I look at my glass and realise I've almost finished it.

'Go on then. V and T please.'

He puts his shopping down and approaches the bar. I'm tempted to look inside, but restrain myself. The present or presents might not even be for me.

Charlie reappears holding a pint of ale and my drink.

'There you go, love.' He slides the tumbler over to me and has a glug from his beer. It leaves a small foam trail on the moustache on his upper lip, which I wipe away with my thumb.

'Any luck with your shopping?' I ask, making a show of eyeing the bag.

'Never you mind.' He takes off his duffle coat and puts it over the carrier.

'Food looks good.' I offer him the only menu on the table. 'Can't decide what to have though. Maybe something light. We're having goose tomorrow.'

'For the three of us? That will keep us going for a week.'

'I wanted to make a special effort this year. What with everything...' my words trail off.

'I'm not saying it's a problem. I love goose. It will be great.'

'You will be nice to her?' I regret asking the question as soon as it's left my lips.

'No. I'm going to be awful. Come on, Jose. Relax. Drink your drink and let's get some food in. I'm starving.'

'Sorry. I know I'm being a nightmare. It's strange. I feel like a teenager again. Introducing a new boyfriend for the first time. It's silly, isn't it? Just ignore me. I'm a prat.'

Charlie looks up from the menu, his eyes smiling.

'Yes you are. But, you're my prat.'

'Thanks. One more thing, please, please, please will you shave before she arrives? You look so much more handsome without the beard. Not to mention younger.'

'O.K.' He scratches his beard as if to say goodbye. 'If it will make you happy.' He puts the menu down on the table. 'I'm going to have a blue cheeseburger.' He claps his hands together, forgetting all about his facial hair.

'It *will* make me happy. Thanks. And so would a goat's cheese salad.' I lean back in my chair and escape into a haze of Christmas carols again.

We finish lunch and wander slowly back to the house. Darkness is beginning to fall and Christmas lights hang between the lampposts.

'Wouldn't it be just great if it snowed?' I hang onto Charlie's right arm and look up at the sky.

'No, it wouldn't, and I don't think it's very likely, anyway. This isn't Victorian Britain nor are we in a Charles Dickens novel.'

'More's the pity.' I refuse to acknowledge him mocking me and check my watch again. It's nearly four in the afternoon. Ailene is meant to be arriving at five. 'We need to get a move on. I still haven't made up the spare bed. Fuck, I hope the sheets are dry in time.' I quicken my stride pulling Charlie along.

'It will be fine.' He is so nonchalant sometimes and it drives me mad.

'I hope you're right.'

We arrive back at the house. Careful not to knock the holly wreath, I unlock the front door to find a small pile of cards dropped through our letterbox. I take them into the sitting room to open and hang on the strings I have hung across the window frame. The card on the top has a red envelope. I tear it open. It is a picture of a robin in the snow and reads Seasons Greetings in gold script. Inside, written in perfect blue ink handwriting, it says,

Dear Josie and Charlie,

Have a Merry Christmas and a Happy New Year.

Best wishes,

CID FLO Kelly Malling.

So, the Family Liaison Office sends cards out to the next of kin of murder victims. I groan, tear up the card and throw it into the waste paper basket. Not today, I think, please not today.

'The bedding is dry.' Charlie calls from the kitchen.

'Great.' I slip off my coat and hang it on the row of hooks in the hallway. 'I'll go and make the bed. Put the kettle on, will you, Charlie? I'd love a cup of tea.'

The phone rings on the small hall table. I reach for the receiver and bring it to my ear.

'Hello?'

'Doll, it's me.' Sophie's voice purrs down the phone.

'Hi. How's things?' I clamp the phone between my ear and my shoulder and take the mug of tea from Charlie in one hand and the folded clean sheets with the other.

'Can't complain. Busy, busy. You?'

'Same here. How are things going with that fella of yours?' I silently hope she is going to tell me she has cut him loose.

'Really well,' she enthuses. 'Couldn't be happier. We are spending Christmas together, just the two of us. Saving all the tedious family stuff for Boxing Day and the New Year. That's why I'm calling, actually.'

'Oh?'

'Just wanted to wish you a Happy Christmas and say I hope it goes well with Ailene.' I've noticed Sophie won't refer to her as my mother yet. I suppose it makes sense, since she grew up thinking of *them* as my parents.

'Thanks. I hope you have a good one too. I'll call you on the 27th for a catch up.'

'Perfect.'

'Sorry, Soph but I've got to go. Things to do. Happy Christmas, friend!'

'You too, Doll.'

The line goes dead and I place the phone back on its receiver. I take a sip of the hot tea and almost burn my mouth. I leave it next to the phone and dash upstairs to make the bed.

When I go into the spare room, it suddenly occurs to me that my adoptive parents never stayed in this house. I never invited them and they never invited themselves. I hope that things with Ailene will be different.

I finish making the bed. I bought some bright pink roses earlier today, arranged them in a flowery jug and put it on top of the pine chest of drawers. I somehow think Ailene will like them. I stand back to view the room. It is small and a bit pokey, but has just enough room for a single bed, the chest of drawers and an old burnt orange velvet Victorian chair, I won on Ebay. Above the bed, hangs a painting I did in Sixth Form, of beach huts along a shore. It's bright and colourful and helps to cheer up the room. The little sash window looks out over our patio. I notice a layer of dirt on the sill, dust it off with my hand, and rub it onto my trousers.

She could be here any minute. I glance at my watch for the hundredth time. I leave the room and rush down stairs to finish my abandoned cup of tea, by now cold.

Charlie is in the sitting room flicking through a newspaper. He has his feet up on the coffee table and I push them off, frowning at him as if I were his mother. He grunts and repositions himself, sitting up higher in his reading chair as I flop down onto the sofa opposite him.

'She'll be here, soon.'

'I know.' He doesn't look up from his paper. 'Bedroom made up?'

'Yep. Spic and span.'

'Right. Now, maybe you can actually relax.' His words are spoken kindly but there is an element of authority in them.

'I will. I will.' I feel harassed by his calmness.

'I'll make a fire.' He folds the paper in two and leans forward, his elbows resting on his knees.

I feel the need to be getting on with something, anything.

'And I'll get the crumpets out of the fridge.'

I leave Charlie on his knees by the wood burner, balling up the pages he wont read of the newspaper and placing them strategically between logs.

I open the fridge and remove the packet of crumpets, but all I want to do is smoke a joint. Just one. But I won't. I don't really want to be stoned when she arrives. I just want to feel comfortable and at ease. I tell myself that the minute she gets here, all these nerves and insecure feelings will melt away. I so hope that will be the case.

Reaching up into the cupboard for the strawberry jam, I realise it isn't there. I start to panic and take all the jars and tins out of the cupboard in my frantic search for it.

'Fuck, fuck, fuck!' I swear aloud.

'What's up?' Charlie's head pokes around the door looking concerned.

'No bloody jam! We're out. We can't have crumpets without jam. What are we going to do?'

Charlie gives a guttural laugh, much to my annoyance.

'I thought something serious had happened.'

'For Christ's sake, it's not funny. She'll be here any minute and we don't have any jam.'

'Josie,' he is standing at full height and looking very serious, 'If you don't calm down, you are going to give yourself an aneurism and me a heart attack. I will finish making the fire then I'll go and get some jam. No big drama. Simple.'

'Sorry.' I feel foolish and apologise.

'Don't be sorry. Just stop being so hectic. Be yourself and everything will be just fine. I promise.' He kisses me and lingers a moment, cupping my face in his large hands. His fingers smell of newspaper ink.

'Thanks. You're wonderful. I don't know what I'd do without you.'

'You're my girl and I love you. Go outside, have a cigarette, then go and watch something mindless on the box. I won't be long.'

'One last thing,' I flutter my eyelashes at him, 'You did say you would shave.'

'I'll go and do that right now, then I'll go out and get the jam. The fire can wait. Don't want your mum thinking I'm a scruff bag.' He touches his hair covered chin.

'Lovely scruff bag.' I reach up and stroke his beard. 'Just for today, yeah? Then you can regrow it. As long as a wizard if you want.' I wink and he pulls a face before disappearing to off to go upstairs and shave.

Half an hour later and I am sitting on the sofa, twiddling my thumbs and trying to enjoy the Kings College

Choir carol service Charlie recorded on the television earlier today. The programme certainly hits the right festive notes but I can't help but clock watch. And then, the front door bell rings.

I jump up out of my seat, turn the television off and run my eye over the living room one last time. I decide it looks tidy and welcoming and turn to answer the door.

I open the door and Ailene is there, clutching a small brown suitcase and a large carrier bag that has presents poking out of the top. She smiles.

'Hello.' She hands me the bag of presents and I have an overwhelming urge to hug her.

'Hi. Come in, please. It's cold out there.'

'It is somewhat nippy.' I like the faint Irish twang in her accent.

'Good journey, I hope?'

'Quite alright, thank you.' She is so polite. I scrutinize her trying to work out why she looks younger. Then it dawns on me.

'You've done something new to your hair.' I stand back a moment regarding the cut and colour. 'I like it. It suits you.'

She blushes and comes into the hallway, pulling her gloves off and rubbing her hands together.

'It's nice and warm in here.' She smiles and beckons to the bag of presents I'm holding. 'Those are for under the tree.'

'Thank you so much.' I put the bag down on the floor and take her coat. 'Can I get you some tea or coffee? Warm you up a bit.' We are both standing slightly awkwardly in the hall, so I pick up the bag and lead the way towards the living room.

'That would be very nice.' She follows me into the room 'Oh my, what a lovely tree.' She goes up to it and clasps her hands together.

'I'm glad you like it.' I feel a warm glow spreading up from my toes. 'So, Ailene,' the sound of her name still feels clumsy on my tongue, 'Tea or coffee?'

'A cup of tea would be lovely.' She sits down in an armchair, her back very straight. I take her bag of presents over to the tree.

'I'll put the kettle on. Make yourself at home. Charlie has just popped out, but he'll be back soon.' I want to put her at her ease and call over my shoulder, 'he's very much looking forward to meeting you.'

I make the mugs of tea in the kitchen and remember from our first meeting, that she has two sugars. Knowing how my Mum takes her tea makes me feel closer to her. I carry the mugs into the living room, smiling. As predicted, all my nervousness has disappeared and I feel like my old self.

'Here you go,' I hand her the tea.

'Ah, perfect, thank you.' She holds it in both hands enjoying the warmth exuding from it. 'So, how have you been?'

'I'm doing well.' And I realise that I am. 'These last few months, as you know, have been very difficult but I feel that now I've turned a corner.'

'That's good.' She bows her head and takes a small sip of tea.

'Awful, awful thing that happened.' Her voice is almost a whisper.

'It is. It was.' I find myself staring into the fireplace, hoping to find warmth from the flames that aren't there. 'But we don't want to dwell on that now.' I sit up and shake my head slightly. 'It's time to look to the future.' I hold my mug up towards her. 'To new beginnings.'

Silently, she lifts her tea up in the air. We look at each other for a moment. Her eyes have a twinkle in them I haven't seen before.

'To you.' Ailene says at last and we drink simultaneously from our mugs. 'Lovely tea,' she says looking around for somewhere to put her mug down.

'On the coffee table is fine.' She reaches for a magazine to put under the mug. She's obvious a coaster person. No ring marks on her furniture, I suspect.

She turns her head slightly so she can admire the tree again. In her profile, I see a reflection of myself. It almost takes my breath away. With each passing minute, I sense myself growing closer to her and it feels wonderful. There is a long comfortable silence as she stares at the tree.

'Just lovely,' she reaches out a hand and caresses a small golden cherub hanging from branch close to where she is sitting. 'Very tasteful.'

'I love Christmas.' I say putting my mug down on the wooden surface of the coffee table without a seconds thought. 'Always have done. Ever since I was little.'

As if I have just slapped her cheek hard, an expression of discomposure flashes across her face to disappear as quickly as it arose. In that moment, I feel the distance flood in between us again.

'Do you like Christmas?' I try to ignore the tension in the air.

'As a Christian, I love Christmas, of course.' Her barriers have gone up and my heart sinks.

Just then I hear the front door and we both stand up.

'Charlie's home.' His timing could not be better. 'Hi.' I call out.

'Damned shops on Christmas Eve. I had to traipse to Tesco on Bethnal Green Road. Can you believe Patel's doesn't sell jam?' He comes into the room dusting off a light smattering of rain from his head and shoulders.

'Oh. Sorry, I didn't realise you'd arrived. How do you do, Ailene. It's very nice to meet you. I'm Charlie.' He moves closer to her, extending a strong hand and gives her his most charming smile.

Charlie stands with his hand out, waiting for her to shake it. He and I watch the hand and Ailene. Eventually, cautious, she takes it, withdrawing hers as fast as she can. Awkward, Charlie retracts his rejected hand to scratch the back of his head.

There is total silence. He turns to look at me and raises his shoulders slightly, confusion clouding his eyes.

'Is everything alright?' I break the silence at last, baffled by the expression on Ailene's face.

'Yes. Of course.' She sits back down in the chair.

'I'll take this through to the kitchen.' Charlie takes quick steps out of the room.

'Are you OK?' I lean toward her speaking in a half whisper.

'Could I have a glass of water?' she looks pale.

'Sure.' She doesn't look well. 'Charlie,' I call out, 'Can you get Mum a glass of water?'

The word slips out without me even thinking about it. She looks at me in shock.

'Oh, I'm sorry,' I feel my cheeks going red. 'I didn't mean...'

'It's fine. I am your mother after all.' There is a small smile on her face.

Charlie reappears holding a tumbler of water and hands it to Ailene before sitting down next to me on the sofa.

'Thank you.' She takes a small sip before putting the glass down on top of the magazine next to her teacup.

'So,' Charlie leans forward to rest his elbows on his knees and tries again, 'we meet at last. It's very nice to be able to put a face to your name.'

His attempt at charm seems lost on her. Another potent pause.

'Tell me a bit about your-self,' she finally responds as though conducting an interview.

'I'm not what you imagined, am I? It's the age thing. Didn't Jose mention it?'

'No, she didn't.' Ailene's reply is cold.

Not understanding why her attitude has changed so fast and why she seems so shaken, I cut in,

'It didn't occur to me.'

'What is the age gap?'

And why the inquisition, I think?

'Eighteen years or thereabouts.' Charlie can't hide his irritation. This meeting is not going the way I thought it would. Ailene fiddles with the small watch on her wrist.

'So, Jose tells me your family are Irish.' Charlie is doing his best to lighten the mood and I reach over and squeeze his knee as a thank you.

'Yes, that's right.' It's like getting blood from a stone. Steely eyes look up and for the first time she makes proper eye contact with Charlie. 'What about you and your family?'

Already, the idea of having her here for Christmas is shaping up to have been a terrible mistake. Bemused, besieged Charlie continues to do his best to please,

'Well, I was born and brought up in Oxford. I have an older sister, who lives in Canada and my younger brother died a few years ago. My mother is still going but the poor old girl is in a home now. She's not well.'

Ailene seems to examine him for a long time. You could cut the air with a knife.

'Is everything alright?' I am worried about her. Her eyes are large and staring and she jumps up from her seat. In slow motion, an expression of utter horror creeps up her face. Her cheeks whiten, her eyes widen.

'No!' she takes a step back, bumping into the Christmas tree and knocking a few decorations off the branches. 'No, it's not! It's impossible.' Her bottom lip is quivering. 'It can't be.'

'What's wrong?' I press her for a second time.

'Charlie?' She puts her hands over her mouth. 'Charles?'

'Do I know you?' He looks to me for help. I shrug my shoulders.

'It can't be.' She looks at the floor, mutters to herself and clasps her head in her hands.

'Are you OK?' I move towards her and try to put my hand on her shoulder but she shrugs me away.

Her brown eyes rise from the floor again and meet Charlie's. He offers a small smile.

'Oh Jesus, Mary, mother of God.' She lurches towards the door, like a possessed woman and I grab her arm.

'What *ever* is the matter? What's going on, Ailene?' I feel the tension in the room closing in on me.

She stops for a moment and tries to compose herself. She straightens her jumper and turns to face at Charlie.

'Skegness, August 1977.'

Her words are full of sadness. I look at Charlie who is now also ashen. It is his turn to step backwards. I know what is coming but cannot believe it.

'Charles,' Ailene's eyes are full of tears. 'You knew me as Ally back then.' Her voice cracks with the whisper.

'No, no. No.' Charlie stands looking at her with terror. 'No. No. You're wrong. No.'

I stand immobilized, holding my breath. Charlie drops the pot of jam he was holding, which smashes onto the floor, glass and red jelly spreading everywhere.

'I'm sorry.' Ailene bows her head.

Before I have had time to react, she has left. The slam of the front door echoes around the house.

Charlie is standing in the same spot, looking at the mess on the floor and shaking his head.

'No. No. No.' He repeats over and over again.

I am shaking all over as I run into the kitchen and throw open the back door. I can't breathe and the cold air hits me in the face like a bullet to my chest. I suck in long, deep, wheezing breaths and stand hunched over, waiting to vomit. But the sickness remains seated, rock-like, in the pit of my stomach.

I come back indoors and run the cold tap, splashing icy water on my face repeatedly to stop myself from feeling faint. It works and I walk, as if through a fog, back into the living room where I find Charlie sitting on the floor in a puddle of jam, glass and tears. He hides his eyes with the palm of his hands, the snot dripping down his face as he sobs uncontrollably. He cannot stand to look at me.

I collapse on the other side of the room, my legs too weak to keep me up.

'Charlie,' my teeth are chattering, 'Charlie, please. Look at me.' But he won't.

'It can't be.' He keeps repeating it over and over again.

Sitting slumped on the floor I gaze at the ruined Christmas tree.

'It can't be.' His words are growing louder and louder.

'SHUT UP!' I scream, putting my hands over my ears. 'Shut the fuck up!'

He stops silent and finally is able to look at me, his tears an extension of the blue in his eyes. Our eyes lock. We sit looking at each other for what seems a long time. A breeze floods in from the open back door, and again I start to shudder.

'Tell me,' I almost choke on the words, 'tell me...'

He drops his head and puts his hands palm down on the floor. I sit, trapped in time, waiting for a reply.

At last he takes his hands off the floor and looks down at the palm on his right hand. A piece of glass is sticking into the round flesh below his thumb. He stares at it for a moment before pulling it out slowly and watching as the blood trickles down his hand, splashing onto the floor.

'I think I am your father.' He says.

Before I've had time to think, I find myself upstairs throwing random belongings into a bag. All I know is that I have to get out of here. I can feel my brain throbbing behind my eyes. I don't remember how I got up the stairs. The sight of our marital bed makes me feel ill. Throwing the tatty, stuffed, satchel over my shoulder, I pull the door closed behind me and stumble into the bathroom. I just have time to get my ginger hair out of my face before I throw up in the toilet. My vomit is a rich pink and the smell of cinnamon swirls around the bowl, forcing me to gag more. Here is the mulled wine I had after lunch.

Getting to my feet and wiping the dribble away from my mouth with my sleeve, I stagger to the sink and take a long drink of water straight from the tap. I cannot bring myself to look at my reflection in the mirror and open the cabinet with my head turned away. Inside, I find a prescription bottle of sedatives, prescribed soon after my parents' murders. I pop the pills into my pocket and drink more from the tap.

Once I'm sure the sickness has passed, I dry my face and leave the bathroom. Standing at the top of the stairs, I listen for signs of life. The house is as quiet as a tomb. I tiptoe down each step, avoid the ones that creak, hoping not to alert Charlie's attention.

As soon as I reach the bottom, I look up to find him slumped against the doorframe. His eyes are bloodshot and he is holding a bottle of whiskey in his hand. I wonder how long I was upstairs for.

'I've got to go. I'm taking the car.' I push past him, grabbing my coat from the hook next to his. We cannot look each other in the eye. I fumble with the Chubb lock on the door and he comes up behind me and puts his hand on my shoulder. I shrug it off. Disgusted by his touch.

'Don't.' My words are as shaky as my hands.

'You can't just leave.'

'I need to get out of here.' The physical closeness of our bodies makes my stomach somersault.

'We have to talk about this.' His words are feeble. Even he doesn't believe in what he's saying.

'I can't do this. I need to get out of this house.' I pull the door open and a biting chill rushes in from the black night.

'Where are you going?'

I fiddle with the keys in the dark, trying to find the car key.

'Anywhere. I don't know! I have to leave. I have to think.' I feel the onset of tears again.

'This isn't our fault. We didn't know!'

His shape is outlined in the doorway, a small man who once appeared large. I glance at him briefly for one last time before disappearing into the night.

I drive in a haze of rain and headlights. The traffic is awful. Crawling through London in the Golf, I keep my eyes on the road while my head goes round in circles.

Before I know what has happened, I find myself driving into Brighton. Without even knowing it, I've ended up outside Sophie's place. But, where else was I supposed to go? I pull the car into a tight parking space and turn the engine off. Resting my head on the steering wheel, I close my eyes as the tears return.

Saliva fills my mouth and the taste of vomit returns. Swallowing it down and wiping my wet cheeks, I get out and lock the car. The street is quiet. I look at the windows in various houses, their lights on and Christmas trees in silhouette. My misery is strangling me as I approach the front door and ring the bell. I really hope she is at home.

'Hello?' Rory's voice calls out from the buzzer. I wasn't prepared to have to face him. It hadn't even occurred to me. I hold my breath for a moment, deciding what to do.

'Hello?' he says again, growing impatient.

'Hi.' I blurt out. 'It's Josie. Is Soph there? I really need to come in.' I wonder if he notices how desperate I sound.

'Em, sure. I'll just buzz you in.'

The noise jumps out of the small speaker and I push the front door open.

When I reach the top of the building, Rory is standing waiting with the door open.

'Hi,' he looks awkward. 'Come in.' I barely notice that his voice is softer than usual. I walk into the flat.

Looking around, I expect to find Sophie but she's not there.

'Where is she?' I rub beneath my eyes, aware that my mascara must be smudged across my face.

'Back soon. Just delivering a present to a neighbour.' He stands with his hands in his pockets, finding it hard to look me in eye. 'Is everything OK?' He knows it isn't.

'I really need to speak to Soph. Is it OK if I wait?' I put my small suitcase down on the floor by my feet and notice him eyeing it. 'I'm sorry to barge in. I just ...' the words escape me.

'It's fine.' He sounds sincere for the first time since I've met him. 'She'll be back soon. Take a seat. Can I get you a drink?'

'Have you got any vodka?'

'Sure do. How do you like it? Ice and lemon?' Rory moves towards the fridge, seeming more at ease.

'No. Straight, please. ' I sit on the edge of the black leather sofa and rub my knees to stop them from tapping.

'Oh, right. Straight it is.' He takes a tumbler out of a cupboard and fills a third of it with the ice-cold vodka straight from the freezer. 'There you go.' I thank him and take the glass. My hand is shaking. He takes a few steps backwards and sits uncomfortably on the edge of a tall stool near the kitchenette.

We share a few awkward, silent minutes until we hear the sound of a key in front door. Sophie's back.

'Rory,' she calls from the hallway shutting the door behind her with a bang, 'Mrs Dorking was thrilled with the chocolates. It was so nice for her to have a visitor,' She comes into the room and stops in her tracks. 'Jose? What are you doing here?'

'I didn't have anywhere else to go.' I can feel my voice cracking as I cling to my cold glass with both hands.

Sophie turns to Rory.

'Be a star, and run to the shop for me, would you?' Her eyebrows are raised in an extreme fashion. 'We forgot to get some chestnuts. '

'Yep. Will do.' Looking so relieved to be excused from the tension, he springs to his feet and rapidly leaves the flat.

Sophie comes over and sits down gently beside me.

'What's wrong, Doll? What's happened?' She slides her arm around my shoulders and pulls me close to her.

Unable to say anything, I burst into tears and bury my face against her bosom.

'Shhh.' She soothes, stroking my hair. 'It's OK. Everything is going to be OK.'

By the time I have finished crying, I am too exhausted to talk. Sophie makes a bed up for me on her sofa and tells me to get some rest.

'We can talk about it in the morning. When you're ready.'

Rory has been hiding in their bedroom ever since he returned from the shop. She turns to look at him and gives a little shrug of her shoulders.

'You can stay as long as you like. We have plenty of food. The more the merrier,' she smiles.

I curl up under a blanket, in the dark and turn away from her.

'Thanks.'

'Sleep well, Doll. I'm sure things will seem brighter in the morning.'

I say nothing and listen to the sound as she closes her bedroom door.

25th December

I wake up and don't know where I am. Then yesterday comes rushing at me like a punch to the stomach.

It's three thirty in the morning and I've only been asleep for a few hours. I swing my legs off the sofa and rub my tired eyes. For a moment, I am able to tell myself that it was just a bad dream. But then I see my bag of hastily packed things, and can no longer escape from the truth.

The large room is cold and dark. I look out at the black night hoping to find some answers in the stars. But there are no stars.

As quietly as I can, I stand and tiptoe across the living room and into the kitchen. Feeling about in the dark, my hand finds the handle to the fridge and I pull the door open. Standing soaked in bright artificial light, I wince as I search for the vodka. It is the only thing that will help me to sleep.

'I keep it in the freezer.' A voice says from behind me and I jump to find Sophie standing there in her dressing gown. There is a sad smile on her face.

'I'm so sorry. I tried not to wake you,' I apologise, feeling my cheeks growing red. I close the fridge door and we are plunged back into darkness. Sophie reaches for the light switch and turns it on.

'You didn't. Get me one, too,' she says yawning, nodding at the freezer and stretching her arms. 'Then let's cuddle up on the sofa, like we used to when we were teenagers and you can tell me what this is all about.'

I nod and open the freezer as she turns and goes over to the sofa. I find two glasses and pour us two large neat vodkas.

I wonder where I will begin. My situation doesn't have a proper story. There is no beginning or end, just that one appalling fact. But how do I begin to actually say it? My tummy rumbles with disapproval as I sip the vodka, hoping to find some courage.

In the living room, I hand her her drink and sit down on the squeaky leather next to her. There is only a small reading light on in the far corner of the room and I am grateful that I can hide from the light.

'So,' Sophie sips the vodka and puffs out her cheeks, 'Are you going to tell me what's going on?'

I put my drink down on the table and bury my face in my hands. A pathetic attempt to hide from her.

'Come on,' she says softly, 'you know you can tell me anything. Is it about Ailene? Did something happen?'

A violent headache is making the blood pound against my skull and I feel as if my brain might explode.

'I can't.' I say feeling dizzy.

'You can.' She puts her hand on my shoulder, encouraging me. 'You can.'

'Charlie is my father.' I say out of the blue, sitting up and looking her.

The confusion on my friend's face is palpable.

'He's my dad.' I say the words as if I am reading them from a book and they have nothing to do with me.

'I'm sorry, I really don't understand,' Sophie looks cautiously at the vodka I am now holding in my hand.

'Charlie is my dad.' I say it again only this time more slowly. The words are foreign to my ears.

'Put the vodka down, Jose. You're not making any sense.' She reaches over and tries to tease the glass out of my hand. All I can do is laugh.

'It's true. Ailene told me. She arrived and when she saw him, she freaked. I didn't know what was happening at first and then she told us she recognized Charlie from all those years ago.'

The nausea returns and I close my eyes in an attempt to escape it. Sophie sits utterly still, trying to process what I have just told her.

'He didn't know either. It was an appalling shock for all of us. Ailene left, and I, well, I couldn't stay there. I didn't know what to do, so I came here.'

When I open my eyes again, the room is spinning.

'Your *father*?' Sophie speaks in a whisper.

'Yes,' I stare at the books on the coffee table, trying to focus on something motionless.

'Are you sure? I mean, is she sure?' I can tell from her tone that Sophie thinks that either I have gone mad or Ailene already is. She doesn't believe what I'm saying.

'Sure.' The word hits me over and over again. 'He remembers meeting her on holiday when they were young. They had sex. She was a virgin. She fell pregnant and they never saw each other again. She didn't touch another man ever again and he never knew she had a baby. Until yesterday.' I am struggling to accept the twisted turn of events.

'But, he's your husband.' Sophie's face is pale. Without realising it, she has moved away from me. I feel the distance between us, growing like mould.

'I know.' My eyes search the floor, unable to look at her any longer. 'He's also my dad. And he's slept with my mum. I can't believe life is so cruel. So fucking unlucky. What are the chances? This isn't a Greek myth. This is my fucking life. '

There is a long, painful silence and I keep staring at the ground, hoping she will say something, anything that might make it better. But she can't.

'Oh, my god.' She stands up and goes over to the window. 'Oh, Christ!'

Please look at me, Soph, I think, *please*. I cannot endure her disgust as well as my own.

She stays by the window with her back to me for what feels like a lifetime. The room is unnaturally quiet and the stillness threatens my sanity.

'Soph?' I know she can feel my eyes staring into the back of her head. She hugs herself as if someone has just walked over her grave. Then very slowly, she turns to look at me. Tears have collected in the corner of her eyes and glisten against the darkness.

'I don't know what to say,' she sniffs trying to hold back the wave of emotion threatening to break through. 'It's just ...' she struggles with her words, '... just so unbelievable.'

'I know,' I say, starting to cry. Normally, Soph would rush over to comfort me but on this occasion she just stands there. 'What am I going to do?' A large trail of snot runs down my face. Now she does. Now she rushes over and holds me. Just like that, she's back, back to being the friend I need her to be.

'Oh, Doll.' She is crying too. My face presses against her dressing gown and a growing wet patch made up of tears and snot. 'It's going to be OK.' She tells us both, trying to sound strong. They are the only words she can manage. 'It's going to be OK.'

The next morning I wake to find Rory sitting quietly on a stool, eating his breakfast on the bar. Frightened to stir and alert him to my waking presence, I freeze and close my eyes again.

Moments later, I hear the bedroom door open and footsteps crossing the floor.

'Morning.' Sophie says to him in a half whisper. 'Happy Christmas.' For a moment I had forgotten what day it was and wish to God it wasn't. I feel even more foolish for being here that I already did. 'She's not awake?' Sophie murmurs quietly. Rory whispers with his mouthful,

'Nope. Not stirred.'

I imagine the chewed toast showing through his teeth.

'Good. She's going to need as much rest as she can get.' Sophie sounds exhausted. 'This is just awful. Poor, poor Josie. Ever since she was a child, she's wanted a proper family. She used to talk about her biological parents as if they were characters from a Disney movie. She had this idea in her head that they were somehow perfect. Now ...' her words melt away.

'Sleep isn't going to make it go away,' Rory says carelessly and I realise that Sophie has already shared with him my dirty discovery.

Unable to bear the thought of listening to them discuss me, I give a loud yawn and sit up on the sofa. I'd rather face them.

'Good morning,' Sophie flashes Rory a look.

'Oh, morning.' He says in a far too cheerful tone. I give a small smile but say nothing and pull the blanket up around myself.

'There's some black coffee in the pot if you want it?' Sophie busies herself, so she doesn't have to look at me.

'No thanks.' I sink back into the sofa and wish I were anywhere else.

'Did you manage to get any sleep?' She tries to sound bright as she pours herself a mug of steaming coffee.

'A bit.' I can't face conversation.

'Want some toast?' Rory waves a slice in my direction. I shake my head and he bites down on it, before turning his back to me again.

'Well,' Sophie is determined to appear jolly, 'in a little while I'll get the smoked salmon and blinis out and we can have some bubbly. How does that sound?'

'Yum.' Rory says still eating toast. Pig.

'That sounds good.'

I get up off the sofa and fold the blanket I slept under. It is their Christmas, after all. It wouldn't be fair for me to ruin it for them, and since I have nowhere else to go, I have to stay and try and make an effort.

'Great.' Sophie flashes me a look of appreciation and readjusts her dressing gown cord. 'I'm going to jump in the bath and then we can get things under way.'

'Soak for as long as you like.' Rory says dusting crumbs off his t-shirt.

'I will.' She kisses the side of his head as she passes on route to the bathroom. 'Why don't you have a bath after me?' She says looking at me. 'Wash away ...' her words fade into nothing. She doesn't know how to finish the sentence and neither do I.

'I will. Thanks.' She shuts the door behind her.

Rory and I are left alone in the huge room with only the sound of running water in the background for company. I've been inside that flat so many times before, but for the first time I feel like an outsider.

Rory tidies his mug and plate away and comes over to the sofa.

'Can I ask you something?' He sits down far too close to me. I hold my breath, dreading the moment he is going to comment on my awful situation. Instead, he removes a small, red, velvet box from his pocket and opens it.

'Do you think she will like it?'

He shows me a dainty diamond engagement ring. I look at it for a while, speechless. Sophie mentioned that marriage had cropped up in their conversations, but I never thought it would happen so soon. Unable to think of an answer, I simply stare at the ring for a while. A small, single diamond sits twinkling in the middle of a yellow gold band.

'Well?' Rory cannot hide his frustration. 'Do you think she will like it?'

I look at him and search his face.

'I'm sure she will.' I cannot muster any real enthusiasm. The truth of the matter is that Sophie does not own any yellow gold jewellery. She doesn't like it. Silver or white gold is her thing. If he really loved her, he would have noticed that. 'Is she expecting it?' I ask as he slides the box back into the pocket of his joggers.

'I hope not.' He winks and I think to myself, what a callous man he is. My marriage has just fallen apart and here he is brandishing an engagement ring under my nose. I'm tempted to bring up the fact that Sophie doesn't like yellow gold, just to take him down a peg or two, but I stop myself, knowing it wouldn't be fair.

'You look after her, OK?' I feel my protective side rear its head.

'I will. Promise.' He says looking at me thoughtfully. Then he pauses as if ordering his thoughts. 'Can I ask you something else?'

'Sure.' I feel uncomfortable under his gaze and shift in my seat.

'Why are you so upset?'

The question completely takes me by surprise.

'I was under the impression Soph had told you,' I choose my words carefully.

'Oh, she has,' he interrupts. I stare at him dumbfounded.

'I'm sorry then, I don't understand.' My face reflects my confusion.

'I just don't really get it.' He says cocking his head to one side. 'You didn't *know* you were sleeping with your dad, so what's the big deal?'

I stop dead and look at him.

'The big deal?'

'Yeah, I mean, if you'd known, you'd have something to feel bad about, but you didn't and neither did he, so,' he pauses, 'it was just a mistake.'

'I cannot believe what I am hearing,' I say shaking all over and moving away from him.

'I'm not meaning to belittle it or anything but, you know, maybe you shouldn't be so hard on yourself.' He explains it the way a child might.

Just then, the bathroom door opens and a cloud of steam erupts out revealing Sophie wrapped in a towel smiling.

'Everything OK?' The smile disappears from her face as she looks at me. 'What on earth's wrong?'

'That man,' I am so angry I might burst, 'that man doesn't see why I might be upset that Charlie is my father.'

'Rory!' Shocked, Sophie's unable to hide her dismay. 'What have you said?'

'Nothing.' Rory holds his hands up in protest as Sophie approaches me with caution.

'I'm sure he didn't mean it like that,' she says trying to keep her towel from slipping down and revealing her naked body.

'All I said was that she shouldn't feel so upset and guilty because she didn't know. I was just trying to help.' Rory looks sheepishly in Sophie's direction.

'Josie, sit down. You are still in shock. I am going to dry myself off and put some clothes on. Just sit here. I'll be back in a minute and then we can talk about it. Forget the stupid blinis and drink. That was a rubbish idea.'

'No, it wasn't.' I say, feeling guilty enough already. 'Please, let's get on with Christmas. Just because mine is a disaster, it mustn't let me spoil yours.' I picture the ring burning a hole in Rory's pocket. Looking at him, I even manage a smile for her sake.

'But Doll, it's too much for you,'

'No,' I interrupt, 'it's not. This problem isn't going anywhere. It'll be the same tomorrow and the day after that. Let's just pretend, just for today that the world isn't a totally fucked up place.'

Sophie almost laughs and then remembers herself.

'Please?'

The couple study me together then nod in unison. It dawns on me that I am looking into the future.

28th December

Christmas day passed, as did the following two days. I had a few missed calls from Charlie but didn't get back to him. I wasn't sure what there was to say.

Rory proposed with the gold ring and she said yes. I feigned happiness for them. It was a good day for Soph.

I stayed with them until the 28th. I couldn't face returning to London until I'd got my thoughts in order. We did a lot of talking, Sophie and I. She was great and as always, so supportive. She told me I would have to go back at some point and face this. Clearly, my marriage was over, there was no other choice, but she said that Charlie and I should grieve the loss of it together. We were both victims, she said. And, of course, she was right. Neither of us knew when we met that we were related. How could we?

We also talked about Ailene. I admitted that the revelation had left me feeling as though I had lost two more parents all over again. How would I ever face her again? How could she ever face me? The whole thing was such a sordid mess that I didn't see any of us ever being able to have a relationship again. We would all have to go our separate ways, in order to leave the mess behind us.

Sophie agreed it was unlikely I would ever be able to see Charlie as my father and that it was probably right if he and I agreed to say goodbye, but her optimistic nature insisted that Ailene and I had a chance of rebuilding a relationship. But I couldn't see the point.

The one good thing that had come as a result of my adoptive parents' deaths was that I had been finally able to move on from the bad things in my past that had so haunted me. I couldn't see a way that I would ever be able to look at Ailene and not see a reflection of my horrible mistake.

I leave in the morning, thanking them both for taking me in and allowing me to gate-crash their Christmas.

'Don't be silly, Doll, you can come back any time." Sophie fiddles with the new ring on her engagement finger. 'I hope it's not too heavy with Charlie. Call me, will you? Let me know you are alright?'

'Of course.' I hug her and for a moment don't want to let go.

'Drive safe.' Rory chips in sliding his arm around Sophie's shoulder.

I get into the car and put the keys in the ignition, waiting to find the courage to start it. Sophie knocks on the passenger window and I roll it down.

'One last thing,' she says biting her gloss-covered lip. 'I know you are going through hell, and I know that's all you can think about at the moment, but I'd love you to be my maid of honour.'

'It would be my absolute pleasure.' I give her the warmest smile I can muster.

'Great. You just take your time to get your life back in order. The wedding can wait a while. There's no real rush.'

'We both know you are going to buy a stack of wedding magazines, the minute you can,' I say grinning, 'and so you should. Be happy. Don't worry about me. I'll be fine.'

'You're the best.' She steps away from the car as the engine roars into life.

'No, you are.' I blow her a kiss and pull out of the parking space. The happy couple stand on the pavement waving me off and I watch them in my rear view mirror until they are out of sight.

The drive back to London is long. Heavy rain slows the traffic to a crawl. I put the radio on hoping to drown out the voices in my head.

Earlier this morning, I had sent Charlie a text letting him know I was on my way back and that I thought we should talk. He hadn't responded but then I suppose I hadn't expected him to. I had ignored his calls after all.

On the drive back, I decide to tell Charlie that he should keep the house and that I will find somewhere else to live. Sophie has a flat in London that she sometimes uses in the week. She offered it to me as a temporary solution and it seems like the sensible thing for me to do. In the back of my mind, I know a large inheritance is waiting for me. At least, I won't have to worry about money. Charlie can keep everything. I don't want a single thing. It would only remind me of what has happened.

As I drive through the busy London streets, watching shoppers rushing from shop sales to shop sales, I play the conversation I plan to have with Charlie over and over in my head. I know I need to keep a calm head. Getting emotional will not help either of us.

I pull onto our street and my stomach does a flip. Coming home used to make me feel so happy. Now, I dread stepping into that house. The place where Charlie and I lived, so happily married. The memory of having sex with him flashes across my mind and my head swims.

I park the car as close to the house as I can, to ensure a quick get away. I turn the engine off. Sitting in the driver's seat, I look out at the small house I used to call home. It looks so normal. If you passed by, it you wouldn't give it a second look. Now, to me it seems like a house of horrors.

Taking a deep breath, I get out of the car and go up to the front door. My keys are in my coat pocket but I feel I should knock. Letting myself in wouldn't feel right, somehow.

I knock loudly once and wait for the sound of approaching footsteps on the other side or the door. There is no answer. I knock again. Don't make me stand out here like this, I think: it's killing me. Again, there is no answer. After trying for a third time and I let myself in.

As I step into the house, I am greeted by a heavy silence.

'Hello?' I call out. No one answers. I push the door closed behind me, shutting out the cold. I hug myself. The house is cold and empty.

I go into the sitting room to find the broken jam jar and its contents still all over the floor. The room looks the same as when I left. I call out again. Nothing.

Where is he? Why isn't he here?

If we aren't going to talk, then I need to collect my things and leave. I look around the strangely silent room, my stare lingering on the knocked over Christmas tree. Then I realise I cannot be in this house a moment longer. I turn and bolt up the stairs, planning to strip our bedroom of everything I need.

As I reach the landing, I stop. A pair of legs dangles from the ceiling. I recognise those shoes immediately. I stand staring at the feet for some time trying to process the sight before me. The feet do not move.

I do not cry out or fall to the ground.

With an unearthly calmness, I tilt my head up to see the rest of the body.

Hanging out of the trap door into the attic is Charlie's lifeless body. His face is in shadow, for which I am grateful, but I know it's him. I turn around and walk down the stairs slowly, watching myself do so.

In the hallway, I pick up the house phone and dial 999.

'What is your emergency?' A nasal voice travels down the line.

'I've just found the body of my dead husband.' I wonder if I am speaking English.

'Your husband has had an accident?' The voice remains steady.

'He's dead.' I feel my mind fracture. 'He's dead.'

When the ambulance and police arrive, I am sitting on the stairs staring into space.

'Are you the lady that called 999?' A pudgy, faced officer asks. He smells like fast food.

'He's up there.' I gesture upstairs and look to the concerned ambulance attendant. 'You're too late.'

The huge man in the racing green uniform clings onto a large medical bag. He pushes awkwardly past me, taking large running strides up the stairs.

'Come on,' the policeman puts his hand on my shoulder,
'Let's go in there.'

He leads me, like a dog, into the sitting room and guides me to the sofa. I notice a large clump of sticky red jam on my shoes. The policeman is speaking into his walkie-talkie, but I cannot process what he is saying.

A moment later, the large ambulance driver appears again. He looks at the police officer and shakes his head quickly, his eyes on the floor, before ducking out.

I sit staring at my hands. They do not tremble. Calmly, I remove my mobile from my pocket and start to search my contacts. Sophie. Call Sophie. It is all I can think.

'Sorry, Ma'am,' the fat faced officer wraps his hand around my phone, 'I'm afraid that will have to wait. Unfortunately, we need to ask you some questions.'

I look up into his chubby face. His shirt is buttoned up to the top, his large neck threatening to burst through at any moment.

He sits down beside me and removes a pad from his pocket.

'Can you tell me your relationship to the deceased, please?' A bead of sweat collects on his brow before rolling down his temple. He doesn't appear to notice that he is sweating.

'I'm his wife.' I stop realising that that isn't the whole truth. 'I mean he's my father.' The policeman snaps his notebook closed and eyes me.

'Sorry, Madam. I think you are a bit confused. Are you his wife or his daughter?'

'I'm both.' I look blankly into his grey blue eyes.

'I didn't know,' I continue unable to stop the flow of words, 'I didn't know when I married him. I was adopted. He didn't know he had a child. We fell in love. I didn't know. Then my parents died. Someone killed them. And I didn't know and then Ailene came into my life. She didn't know, until she met him. She was horrified. She told us what we were to each other. I didn't know.'

I am losing control of the speed of my speech and can hear each syllable growing louder. The policeman tilts his round head to one side and examines me.

'OK. You are in shock. That's obvious. I'm going to start again. I want you to take a deep breath and answer my next question, as clearly as you can, OK?' His cockney accent is thick and soothing. 'Can you please tell me the name of the deceased?'

'Charlie Brewers.' The words leave my mouth slowly.

'OK,' the Bobby opens up his pad again and jots that down, 'that's good. Now can you tell me the age of the deceased?'

'He was fifty-five in May.' Now, my hands are beginning to shake and I can feel the blood draining from my face. The policeman stops for a minute, noticing the change in my expression.

'OK. Can you tell me when you discovered the body?'

'Just before I called 999.' This line of questioning seems so pointless. 'I didn't see his face. I couldn't look. But I know it's him. I know it's Charlie. I recognise his shoes.' My voice trembles.

'Right. I'm going to get you a glass of water. I want you to wait here. Don't move all right? I'll be back in a tick.'

I don't respond but remain seated. I couldn't move even if I wanted to.

He picks himself up, his large frame resisting and walks out into the hallway. That's not the way to the kitchen I think but remain silent. From the hallway, I can hear whispered voices. The ambulance man pops his head around the corner to take a quick look at me before disappearing again and the whispers continue.

The policeman comes back into the room accompanied by the ambulance driver.

'He's going to fetch you some water, OK?' He smiles, gesturing in the direction of his companion who follows his instruction and heads off towards the kitchen. I hear another car pull up outside. Two more officers walk into the house and take themselves upstairs.

Moments later, I am handed a tall glass of water. I drink it all in one go.

The policeman says,

'I'm terribly sorry but I'm afraid we need to ask you to view the body.' He scratches his chubby, sweaty neck with his pen. 'Since you told me you did not actually see his face, we do need a formal identification. I know this is going to be difficult for you. You can take your time. He's been laid out on the bed. Just let me know when you're ready and I'll come up with you.'

The room starts to spin. Faster and faster. His face looms closer as darkness begins to absorb the light.

'Madam?' I can feel his hand on my shoulder again but am unable to respond.

'In here!' he calls out. Two uniformed officers appear along with the ambulance man who was first on the scene. 'I think she's going to faint.' The officer sounds weary.

The large ambulance driver gets down on one knee and shines a torch in my eyes. I don't blink.

'Miss?' he speaks softly, 'Miss?'

Suddenly as if someone turned a light on in my head, I am brought back to earth.

'Miss, are you OK?' his face is kind and I notice the deep lines in his forehead for the first time. This cannot be an easy job.

'Yes. I'm sorry. I felt really dizzy but I'm OK, now.' The police officer looks at his colleagues and shrugs.

A small officious woman stands impatient in the doorway.

'I'm sorry, but we do need to get an ID.'

'Alright.' I stand up. My legs might buckle. They don't. 'I'm ready.'

When I go into our bedroom, I notice how still everything is. The birds have shut up. The sirens have fallen quiet. The world seems at peace.

The kind-faced ambulance driver is standing next to the bed, his hands clenched in front of him.

I do not look at the body covered by a blanket. I know it's there. Not realising I'm holding my breath, I nod at the officer standing by my side, probably waiting to catch me. The ambulance driver whose name I now know is Dirk, carefully folds back the top of the blanket to reveal a man's face.

His skin is the colour of stone. Any expression that used to be there has long gone. It is a body now, nothing more. An empty vessel lying marooned in this unnatural position. Horrified and fascinated by what I see, I step towards the corpse. His mouth is slightly ajar and in the corner of his lips, a small amount of blood has collected and dried. Somehow though, he looks peaceful.

It doesn't look like Charlie. I move closer still, just to be sure. But it is. I hardly recognise this pale, lifeless thing laid out on the bed. My hand trembles as I run my fingers through his hair.

'It's him.' I say, unwilling to look away from his face. 'It's Charlie.'

January 8th

I decide not to go the funeral. There will be too many people there who think of me as his wife, telling me how wonderful he was and how much he loved me. The truth hasn't got out, yet. I don't suppose it needs to, now.

I have had to endure the endless phone calls and sympathetic letters telling me what a surprise and a tragedy his death has been. Like the dutiful wife, I've listened to his friends recount stories from the past, anecdotes about how full of life he was. It's all true, all of it. But I don't feel it anymore.

Charlie died on Christmas day. He drank a whole bottle of whiskey and then hung himself from a beam in the attic. The coroner pronounced his death as a suicide. Soon afterwards, I was expected to arrange the funeral.

The police put my answers to their questions on the day down to shock. I didn't confess what I knew had led him to do it. It would dirty his memory. I didn't want that for him and truthfully, I didn't want it for myself. He died a loyal, loving husband and that was how it should be. The world didn't need to know the awful truth. It wouldn't help anyone.

The day after I discovered his body, I called Sophie and told her. She jumped in her car and came up to London immediately. She has been staying with me and has been so helpful, clearing up all the mess, cleaning and tidying the house until this morning, when I told her she had done more than enough for me and that she should return to Brighton. Resentfully, she agreed. She hid it well but I could tell she was missing Rory.

The final thing I asked Sophie to do before she left was to represent me at the funeral today. I asked her to explain to everyone that I was simply too upset to attend. Being the wonderful friend that she is, she readily consented. Nothing is ever too much trouble. She is the only person left in my life whom I can truly rely on.

She had been the one who convinced me to call Ailene and tell her what had happened. I couldn't face it, but knowing that I was determined to persevere with the charade, Soph pointed out I needed to get Ailene to agree to keep quiet.

Ailene had immediately concurred that it would be best for all concerned for the truth to remain buried. No one ever need know, she said. But I knew and she knew and that was enough to make me hate myself. It also became clear that she and I stood no chance of building a relationship.

I told her when the funeral was and that was the last conversation I had with her. She sounded sad. She was distant and formal and I thought it would be the last time I ever spoke to her.

Standing in the living room of the house, I shared with Charlie, through the window I watch Sophie get into her car and drive away to the crematorium. From there, she will go straight back to Brighton. We agreed it would be very awkward to see each other again afterwards.

I may not be going to the funeral but that doesn't mean I don't feel like wearing black. I am wearing the same black dress I bought for my adoptive parent's funeral, and the irony is not lost on me. I didn't think that I would be wearing it for Charlie first.

It is only 11.00 a.m. in the morning but I pour myself a large glass of white wine, anyway. I need something to help me get through. I try not to imagine the crowds of people preparing to attend Charlie's funeral.

Being in this house, where I learnt that he was my father and where I discovered his body, hurts so, so much. Every item reminds me of Charlie and our lives together. As soon as a good memory (there are so many) stirs, it is ripped away to be replaced by the recollection of our last afternoon spent together; that awful afternoon that changed everything and led to the death of the man I loved.

I decided a few days ago, that while the funeral was taking place, I would pack up my things and disappear. Sophie reiterated that her London flat was still on offer. I would leave my mobile behind and turn my back on a life that had included Charlie.

I had never wanted to remain here, for even one day with the ghost who lingered there, but if I was going to keep up appearances, I needed to remain a little longer. I kept reminding myself that it wasn't forever and taken one day at a time, Soph's presence helped.

Apart from Ailene, Sophie and Rory were the only two who knew about my biological relationship to Charlie. Sophie had thoroughly reassured me that they would never utter a word to anyone. She had never lied to me before and I had no reason to doubt her now.

I went from room to room, looking at the objects that belonged to a life I no longer recognised. Pictures of Charlie and I smiling, trinkets we'd bought on holiday, presents we had been given for our wedding; a lifetime of possessions that now meant nothing. I shall leave them all behind. A house clearance company can come and have their fill. Then the house will be put on the market and I shall be rid of all the material things that link me to my appalling secret.

As I come back down stairs carrying a box full of my things, the house phone rings. I put the box down and check my watch. It's eleven thirty and the funeral begins in half an hour.

'Hello?' I answer gingerly, not wanting to face any of the other mourners.

'Hello.' I identify her voice immediately.

'Ailene?'

'Yes. I'm sorry to call now, I'm sure you're on your way out.' She can't bring herself to mention the funeral. 'I just thought you should know that I am going to be there.'

'Where?' I am confused.

'The crematorium.' She says quietly. 'I hope you don't mind. It just felt wrong staying away. I'll slip in the back. No one will notice me. I won't say a word.'

My shoulders drop.

'It's fine. You go.' I look down at the small box containing my personal effects. 'I'm not going.'

'Why?' her voice goes up a pitch.

'Because, I can't face it and I can't pretend anymore. I've done everything I can to preserve his memory but I cannot go and sit and cry and talk to all the people who knew us the way we were. I can't do it.' I sit on the bottom stair slumped, still holding the phone. All the energy has left my body. 'I'm moving out as we speak. I can't be here a moment longer.'

There is a silence.

At last, she says,

'Let me come and see you, after. This is all my fault.'

Her last statement rings in my ear. She is right. It *is* her fault. Everything.

'Ok.' I agree, wondering what there is left for us to say.

'Promise me, you'll wait for me to arrive? I'll come straight to you. I have no business being at the wake.'

'OK. I'll still be here.' An instant headache has hold of my brain and white spots dance in front of my eyes. 'See you later.' I hang up the phone.

I wait for the white spots to disappear and for the headache to subside a little. Then, I get up, kick the box out of the way with my foot and return to the living room where the dried out skeleton of the fallen Christmas tree lies broken on the floor, telling our story. I wonder why I didn't throw it out before.

"It is all my fault."

Her words are whirling around my mind and gathering speed. I pace backwards and forwards, nearly wearing a groove in the floorboards. With a sudden jolt I remember the rucksack under our bed. I have a desperate urge for a cigarette. I grab my coat and bag, slip my boots on and pull the front door closed behind me.

When I get to the door, I'm not surprised to find it's on the latch. People are still pretty fuckin' careless, I think, pushin' it open. As I step in, I know there's no one in the house. It's quiet as a tomb. I don't wipe my feet or nothin'. So what if it's been rainin' and the pavement is awash? There are more important things for me to be worryin' about right now.

The place is dark. There's not a light on anywhere and the January weather is doin' nothin' to brighten it up. On the floor in the hall in front of me is a box full of ladies' things. I get down on my haunches and go through it.

There's a mirrored box of jewellery. I open it and look at the collection of bracelets and earrin's all tangled in a mess together. This person needs to take better care of her things. I close the lid and drop it back into the box. Then I take out a small leather book. It's worn and old and the leather feels like butter in my fingers. Embossed on the front, in small faded gold writin' is the word 'Diary.' I think about openin' it but I don't. I've got no business pokin' about in some woman's deepest, darkest thoughts. It won't tell me anythin' I don't already know, anyway. I put it back and pick up a jade green scarf. It smells like roses and freshly made biscuits. I bury my face in the soft fabric and breathe in long and hard.

After lookin' through the rest of the box and decidin' there's nothin' worth keepin', I go upstairs to have a look about.

The house annoys me. It's decorated in a sort of hippy way I don't like. Why do people insist on packin' their lives full of clutter? I knock a picture off the wall as I pass it. The glass cracks and the frame smashes on the floor. A picture of a smilin', happy couple lies broken on the landin'.

Next, I go into one of the bedrooms. I notice how tidy it is compared to the rest of the house. There isn't any clutter in here apart from some dead flowers in a vase. The bed is made up, and it feels a bit like a hotel room that hasn't had anyone stay in it for a while. I go into the room next door. It's a real mess. I go over to the wardrobe and flick through the clothes. There is a bunch of men's shirts hangin' in it. I hate city workers. Wankers, the lot of them. This fella certainly doesn't share my idea of what to wear. But he's older than me. I know that.

I go over to the un-made bed and sit on it, bouncin' slightly up and down and gettin' used to the softness of the mattress. I become aware of the dampness of my trousers. The smell of dirty rain fills my nostrils. It takes me back to bein' in the woods before...

I am reminded of why I came up here and I get down on the floor. It's odd bein' there, so low on the ground, like a slug. You get a different point of view from down here, like bein' a kid again.

Then I reach under the bed and pull the bag out. That is what I came here for.

I throw it over my shoulder and go back downstairs, treading the broken glass from the picture into the carpet as I pass by.

Once downstairs, I make myself at home on the sofa. It's dark in this pokey, little livin' room and I reach over to turn a lamp on. That's better. Now I can actually see.

I put my rucksack on the floor, unzip it and remove an object that I lay out on the coffee table in front of me. I look at it and smile. Everythin' has come full circle.

I'm bored while I sit waitin' for her to arrive. The minutes go by slowly as I watch the hands on the clock makin' their way around the face. I pick up a magazine from the table and flick through, just to pass some time. It's a Christmas catalogue full of photos of smilin' brats and their parents' sittin' in showroom houses next to their perfect fuckin' Christmas trees. I wonder if anythin' real is ever for sale. I turn page after page filled with crap gifts like a fish shaped bottle opener, personalised cufflinks, gadgets for the kitchen that are no use to anyone. I crumple it up and throw it on the ground.

Where is this stupid bitch?

Then, as if by magic, I see a figure pass by the window. I know it's her. This is the moment I've been waitin' for. I stand up, pick up the thing on the coffee table and arrange myself so I'm standin' with my back to the door. I made sure I left the front door wide open so that she'd stroll in. I didn't want her knockin'. It would be better this way.

I take a deep breath and puff my shoulders up, sensin' she is now standin' in the room.

'Hello?' Her voice is tentative.

'Hello.' I echo, not turnin' round.

'I'm here to see Josie. Is she here?'

'No, she's not,' I say turning round, 'but I am.'

The woman looks at me for a moment, confusion and horror both fightin' for a place on her face.

'I'm sorry, I don't understand. Why are you dressed like that?' she holds her hands out in front of her.

'I think there are more pressin' questions,' I say removin' the metal object from behind my back.

Her sunken eyes widen when she sees what I'm holdin'. They fix on the cold, hard, metal of the crowbar and linger there.

'What are you doing?' The fear is her voice is intense.

'Nothin' yet. I think we should have a chat first.' I say, steppin' towards her, grippin' the weapon in my hand so tightly that it feels like I'm cuttin' off the blood supply.

'Josie, please,' she begs stumbling backwards, 'I don't understand.'

I stop and take a look at the frightened wreck standin' in front of me.

'Josie ain't here.' I lift the crowbar high above my head and bring it crashin' down onto the coffee table.

'Oh, my God,' she whispers under her breath before turnin' and runnin' out of the house.

I stand there watchin' her go. I don't stop her.

I think about runnin' after her, she wasn't meant to get away, but I've changed my mind. It's over now. Everythin's over.

I put the crowbar down on the sofa and go into the kitchen. Methodically, I take out every bottle of booze I can find and every cleanin' liquid and line them all up on the side.

One by one, I take off the lids and pour them in circles all over the kitchen. Then I move into the sittin' room carryin' the rest and do the same. The place smells like it belongs to an alcoholic with O.C.D. I kind of like it.

With the last bottle of Scotch, I lay a trail of liquid on the floor and move backwards, towards the front door, emptyin' it as I go. Then, without a second's hesitation, I pull a box of matches out of my pocket and light the alcohol. I watch for a minute as a pathway of angry flames rush away from me and into the rest of the house.

Steppin' out into the fresh air, I take a deep breath and close the door as the sound of fire roars up behind me. Then, with my hands in my pockets, I wander over to the pavement on the other side of the road, sit down and watch as the flames grow and envelop the house.

Out of the corner of my eye, I catch sight of my reflection in a puddle. The ripples in the water disturb the image. When the surface settles I look down at myself and see Josie's face smilin' back at me.

January 12th

I wake up with a splitting headache. My whole body is throbbing. I don't open my eyes for some time, waiting for the pain to ease, which it doesn't. The bed I'm lying in feels strange, harder than usual and I can smell something odd. Gingerly, I sit up and rub my eyes. I notice my hands smell of booze and smoke. But not cigarette smoke; bonfire smoke.

When I open my eyes I am in a place I don't recognise and I'm wearing a hospital gown. I look around the small room trying to find something that will indicate where I am.

There is one small window, high up, with a grate across it. Apart from the bed and one small chair in the corner, the room is bare. I pull the scratchy blue blanket away and get out of bed. My legs are wobbly as I go over to the door. I search for a handle or doorknob. There isn't one. I can't open the door from my side.

Where am I?

I bang my fists on the metal door.

'Hey! Anyone there? Get me out of here! Please?' I stop and listen for signs of life. 'Hey! What the fuck? Let me out!'

A small window in the door slides open and I see a pair of blue eyes staring back at me.

'You want me to get a doctor?' The man on the other side asks, chewing gum.

'Doctor? Of course, I don't want a doctor. I want to get out of here. Now!'

Intimidated by the cold stare, I back away.

'Fine. Stop banging on the door. I'll get someone to come see you.' He pulls the shutter back across the opening again.

I go back to the bed and sit down. None of this makes any sense.

How did I get here? Why am I here?

I wait for some time before I hear the click of the door unlocking. I get up and straighten my gown, hoping to feign some semblance of respectability.

A man comes in accompanied by two males wearing male nurses' uniforms. They are both huge. What sort of joke is this? The nurses stand guarding the door, one black, and one white. The man, who at a guess, is in his fifties, fiddles with the glasses on his face with one hand while holding a file in another.

'To whom am I speaking, today?' He asks, looking at the paperwork in his file. He doesn't look me in the eye.

'What do you mean "to whom am I speaking?" My name is Josie Brewers. Can you please explain to me, what the hell you are talking about, what the hell this place is and why I appear to be under lock and key?'

Part of me thinks this is just a strange dream.

'Right, OK then. Josie,' He closes his file and points to the chair. 'Do you mind if I take a seat?' He behaves as if we are old friends about to share coffee and doughnuts.

'Be my guest.' I stand, arms crossed, waiting for him to sit down before backing up towards and lowering myself onto the bed.

'I am Dr Luke King. This is a psychiatric hospital. You were brought in here last night,' He leans forward, 'but you don't remember?'

'Psychiatric hospital!' Oh, God. 'No.' I scratch my head. 'Not a thing.'

'Do you know anyone called Jacob?' He holds his chin in one hand, sits back in his seat and tips his head slightly to one side.

'It doesn't ring any bells.' I answer honestly.

'OK.' He leans forward again and fixes me with his small green eyes. 'This is a delicate matter that I wish to handle with care.' I scream in my head, *stop pontificating and tell me what's going on*. 'When you arrived yesterday, you told me your name was Jacob.' He stops talking and looks at me for a reaction.

'That's absurd!'

This has to be a dream.

'It sounds absurd, I know but it isn't exactly. When I met you yesterday, you said you were called Jacob. You spoke with a completely different accent. You appeared to be a completely different person.'

I look at the nurses guarding the door waiting for them to burst into laughter and for someone to pop their head around the corner and yell "Gotcha!"

'It has become clear after speaking to a …' he checks the notes in his file, '… DS Woolfson of the Gloucestershire Police, that you are suffering from an illness known as D.I.D, which stands for Dissociative Identity Disorder'

'I'm sorry?' I jump off the bed and look at him dumbfounded. 'Can you please tell me what the fuck you are talking about?'

'Josie, please sit down.' I feel the presence of the nurses growing nearer.

'OK, OK.' Angry, I do as he says.

'D.I.D. Are you familiar with the illness?'

'No, I certainly am not.' *What is he talking about?*

'Until recently, it was called Multiple Personality Disorder.'

'So, you're telling me I'm nuts. Do I have that right? That sometimes I think I'm a guy called Jacob?'

'No, you are not nuts, you are ill, Josie.' He looks very serious. 'I am sorry to break such bad news to you but it appears that this other personality you harbour has been responsible for some very serious crimes.'

'This really is nuts.' I want to laugh but don't. I glance at the nurses. Do they find this funny? Apparently not.

'Jacob was arrested outside your house,' he continues, paying no attention to my last statement, 'after starting a fire. He was taken to the local police station, where he then admitted to committing a double murder.' The doctor pauses for a minute and allows the information to sink in. I cannot process what he's telling me, but somewhere deep down, I recognize the truth of it. 'You have another personality called Jacob, Josie. And Jacob murdered Fiona and Harold Griffin.'

I feel glued to the bed. I don't know where to look. A cold chill from somewhere comes in through the open door. I look down at my hands and tell myself this isn't real. But it is.

'I didn't kill anyone.' It's all I can think to say.

'No,' he gets up out of the chair and comes over to the bed where he quietly sits down next to me, 'you didn't.' His voice is full of sympathy. 'But Jacob did.'

'I don't understand.' The tears stream down my face and I turn to look at him. He has kind eyes and an expression full of pity. He gently puts his hand on my lap.

'You have been put here under my care.' His voice is gentle, soothing. 'Together, we are going to work out what led to this and what happened to cause this illness.'

'How long do I have to stay?' My body is flooded with fear.

'I can't answer that question yet, I'm afraid.' His face tells me there is more but I don't want to hear it.

'This is an especially complicated situation, given your current physical state.'

'What do you mean?' I wipe the tears away from my face. He stands up and moves a few feet away from me.

'You are five months pregnant.'

April 19th

It's been a few months since I first came here. So much has happened since then. I've had so much to come to terms with. I still can't really believe it.

After many hours spent talking to Dr King, we have established why I have this illness. It stems from my childhood, from the years of sexual abuse I suffered. Dr King suspects that my mind invented Jacob, as a means of escape. Jacob is tough and strong. Jacob is not a victim. Unlike Josie, unlike me, Jacob can handle himself.

It makes sense, in a twisted sort of way that this other person exists. What I can't come to terms with is the violence he brings with him. Why did he have to kill them?

In order to help me come to terms with the existence of Jacob, Dr King showed me a video recording of myself when I'm him. It was bizarre to watch. All this time there has been a whole other person living inside me. The Doc thinks it's quite possible there might be others. That's something else he wants us to investigate in therapy.

I am going to have to stay here for the foreseeable future. I can't be released in case Jacob shows up and starts causing trouble. It's possible that one day I will be able to live without him, but until that day arrives, I have to stay in the hospital. It's got to be better than prison though, so that's something.

When I learned I was pregnant, it made me feel ill. They offered me an abortion. Apparently, you can have a late one if you've been raped or the foetus is a product of incest. The word alone makes me want to scratch it out of my stomach.

They had to do a scan before anything else. That sealed the deal. The moment I saw the outline of the child's little body on the screen, its tiny arms and legs moving around, I knew I couldn't go through with it. Whatever my relationship to Charlie was, this was his child too.

I spent a long time talking through what my options were. Obviously, I can't raise a child in here and I wouldn't want to. As much as I couldn't bear to abort the baby, I cannot allow myself to dream about bringing it up. What sort of mother would I be, knowing what I am, who the boy's father was and all that has happened?

Sophie was allowed to visit me a while ago. I sat and talked it all through with her. She's been amazing this whole time. She is the only person in my life who's never let me down.

She has offered to look after the child. She said she and Rory had talked it through and had decided they would love to raise and nurture it. To begin with, I was dead against the idea. I hardly know Rory and don't especially like or trust him. But, I have little choice and it seems to be the only option. Knowing what I do about what can happen to adopted children, I didn't want someone unknown to take my baby. I know Sophie so well and love her so much, as she does me and I am certain she will do a wonderful job raising the child. I owe her so, so much.

There have been a lot of legal problems with the will. The laws states that no one should benefit financially from the death of someone they have killed. However, *I* didn't kill my parents, *Jacob* did. Sophie put me in touch with a lawyer friend of hers who has dealt with it all for me.

It was agreed that the inheritance would go into a trust for my child, which was sensible. Soph and Rory will get a financial monthly contribution to help pay for his upkeep. From a twisted, messy situation, things have worked out as well as can be expected.

I look down at my large belly and rub where I'm being kicked from inside.

'Hey sport, stop that.' I say out loud.

When I had the scan, I was asked whether I wanted to know the sex of the child. I did as did Soph and Rory and I am having a boy.

Sophie says Rory is over the moon since "teaching and being with boys is what Rory enjoys most about his job."

We have negotiated with the hospital to allow Soph and Rory to be here for the birth. They will be here when he comes, and then they will take him away.

I've had lots of tests to track the progress of his development in the womb. So far, nothing bad has shown up. I just pray he isn't brain damaged or something.

Sophie and Rory were married last week. They wanted it to be finalised before the arrival of what will become their son. Obviously, I couldn't go to the wedding, a thing I found really hard to accept. But she's so sweet, she sent me pictures in the post. She looked stunning in her long cream satin gown and so happy. I put them up on my bedroom wall and look at them every day.

Sometimes, the thought of ordinary life going on outside without me in it makes me very sad. But then I look down at my tummy and remember there is life in here, too.

September 28th

I've been here for a long time now. I know the names of all the staff and even manage to have a laugh and a joke with some of them on occasion. They're not all bad.

I have to talk to the doc a lot. He's the first person who's really showed an interest in me. I like it. It's about time I was recognised and people paid attention.

The food in this place fuckin' stinks. That's the worst thing about it. Other than that it's all right, I suppose. There's a games room at least. I've got good at table tennis.

They told me off once for threatenin' someone else who's locked up in here. The cunt wouldn't stop laughin' at me. Kept callin' me a girl. I wanted to bash his face in with the bat. They stopped me playin' for a while but I promised to be good. Some people will believe anythin' you tell them.

The doc told me that my "victims" were finally buried. As if I give a fuck. Still, I'm happy in the knowledge that that animal was buried without his head. Sometimes, they ask me where I put it. But I won't tell. It's my little secret. He won't be needin' it where he's goin'.

Now that Josie knows about me, it feels like I've come out of the shadows. She doesn't need me now, not like she used to. It's not easy but it's somethin' I've got to accept. I'll keep an eye out for her still. I always will. I'm never goin' to leave her. Not ever.

Taken from www.psychologytoday.com

Sources

- American Psychiatric Association
- National Institute of Mental Health
- *Handbook of Psychology*, Vol. 8 (John Wiley)

Definition of Dissociative Identity Disorder

Called Multiple Personality Disorder until 1994, the name was changed to reflect a better understanding of the condition—namely, that it is characterized by a fragmentation, or splintering, of identity rather than by a proliferation, or growth, of separate identities.

Dissociative Identity Disorder (DID) is a severe condition in which two or more distinct identities, or personality states are present in — and alternately take control of — an individual. The person also experiences memory loss that is too extensive to be explained by ordinary forgetfulness.

DID is characterized by identity fragmentation rather than a proliferation of separate personalities. The disturbance is not due to the direct psychological effects of a substance or of a general medical condition, yet as this once rarely reported disorder has become more common, the diagnosis has become controversial.

DID reflects a failure to integrate various aspects of identity, memory and consciousness in a single multidimensional self. Usually, a primary identity carries the individual's given name and is passive, dependent, guilty and depressed. When in control, each personality state, or alter, may be experienced as if it has a distinct history, self-image and identity. The alters' characteristics — including name, reported age and gender, vocabulary, general knowledge, and predominant mood — contrast with those of the primary identity. Certain circumstances or stressors can cause a particular alter to emerge. The various identities may deny knowledge of one another, be critical of one another or appear to be in open conflict.

Causes

Why some people develop DID is not entirely understood, but they frequently report having experienced severe physical and/or sexual abuse, especially during childhood. Though the accuracy of such accounts is disputed, they are often confirmed by objective evidence. Individuals with DID may also have post-traumatic symptoms (nightmares, flashbacks, and startle responses) or Post-Traumatic Stress Disorder. Several studies suggest that DID is more common among close biological relatives of persons who also have the disorder than in the general population. As this once rarely reported disorder has grown more common, the diagnosis has become controversial. Some believe that because DID patients are easily hypnotized, their symptoms are iatrogenic, that is, they have arisen in response to therapists' suggestions. Brain imaging studies, however, have corroborated identity transitions in some patients.

Treatments

The primary treatment for DID is long-term psychotherapy with the goal of deconstructing the different personalities and uniting them into one. Other treatments include cognitive and creative therapies. Although there are no medications that specifically treat this disorder, antidepressants, anti-anxiety drugs or tranquilizers may be prescribed to help control the mental health symptoms associated with it.

Acknowledgements

Many thanks to Detective Superintendent Brian Foster and Detective Sergeant David Fuller for helping me to keep the details based in reality. Thank you to my husband for keeping me sane and to my children for keeping me smiling. It goes without saying that I could not have finished this book without the support of all the brilliant people in my life. Last but not least, a huge thank you to my editor.

17582979R00125

Printed in Great Britain
by Amazon